Race
for the
Topaz Stallion

K. M. STEELE

HAWKEYE
PUBLISHING

First published in Australia in 2024 by Hawkeye Publishing.
Copyright © K. M. Steele.

Cover Design by Ellen Milligan

A catalogue record of this book is available from the National Library of Australia.

ISBN 9781923105225

Proudly printed in Australia.

www.hawkeyebooks.com.au

Praise For RACE FOR THE TOPAZ STALLION

'Another knock-out from Steele! The Mallory Cash series mixes crazy cops-and-robbers action with genuine heart. Full of humour, world-travelling adventure, and beautiful scenery, this book refuses to be put down.'
Nita Delgado, Editor

'Steele's thrilling action-adventure sequel is fast-paced and sassy. The interplay between law and outlaw, and trust and distrust pulls Mallory Cash around the world in a race to find family, love, and answers.'
Beth Falzon, Reviewer

'A fantastic sequel to *Hunt for the Virgin Rainbow* that sees a change of fortune for Mallory and Sam, and offers the reader plenty of adventure, action and backstory.'
Grace Lila, Artist

'Racy, pacy and sassy, I enjoyed this book immensely. Standouts for me are Steele's humour that infuses the narrative. And the backstory in this instalment of the series is satisfying and revealing. Highly recommended.'
Cate Sawyer, Author

To my sons, James and Sam,

for putting up with it all.

1

JIMMY the Cat's shark grin was still visible to the couple below as the chopper ascended out of the gorge. He gave a small wave, like a royal bestowing a parting gift to his subjects. Mallory's chest tightened in fear, her breath coming in short, panting gasps, her fists clenching as the aircraft disappeared behind the wall of the gorge. She wished, in that moment, she had a gun and could have dispatched Jimmy for good and all. The silence that followed the thunder of the departing helicopter filled the gorge, causing the anxious pressure in her chest to tighten another notch.

She was unaware that Sam was watching the emotions flit across her face. When he pulled her deeper into his arms, she felt his head shift to look at the empty sky above.

'I'm sorry, I wasn't entirely truthful,' he said. His arms tightened, and his eyes were wary as she turned her face up to his. 'We can't go after Jimmy the Cat,' he continued, 'I didn't want you to do something you'd regret while he was still here.' He glanced toward the house at the end of the gorge. 'I'll be quick. You know my sister doesn't know the whole story about you.'

Mallory pushed his arms off, her face expressionless.

He shook his head. 'Come on, Mal, you know I have to go to Sydney tomorrow. That's been arranged for months. Your handlers are already on their way.'

She folded her arms. 'And *you* know that now that Jimmy has found me, I can't stay here. I must find my father.'

He frowned. 'Don't be stubborn. Going to Europe is not even a remote possibility. If by some miracle you could get there, you would expose yourself – and possibly your father – to Jimmy.' He stepped away from her, running his hands through his hair in exasperation. 'And what about your old boss, Trafford, or his ex-wife, Eve? They will come after you too.'

She shrugged. 'Jimmy knows where I am. Trafford won't be far behind.'

Sam sighed, his frustration evident. 'You know you'll be moved now. It will be cleared with your handlers before they arrive tomorrow.'

'So that's it? End of story?' He reached for her hand, but she pulled back, eyes flashing. 'You said I wouldn't have to go alone! You said you would help me. I thought—' Her throat constricted. She stopped before angry tears betrayed her.

He dropped his hand and studied her face. Mallory tried to keep her expression impassive, but she knew her eyes burned with anger.

'I'm sorry. The only place you're going to is another safe house,' he said. 'While I'm in Sydney, I'll see what I can dig up. Jimmy is on the move. I'll access Interpol and find out what I can.'

Mallory's expression softened and his tension eased. 'Just play by the rules, please. I'll sort it out.'

She gave a slight nod. 'Okay.' She turned her head to stare at the empty sky, still tracking the invisible trail where the helicopter had departed.

While Mallory contemplated the sky, Sam stepped closer, bridging the gap that had grown between them as the conversation progressed. She lifted a hand and pointed at an eagle hovering near the end of the gorge. Sam smiled and touched her shoulder, releasing a long breath. The tension that had building in her relaxed. It seemed he trusted her after all.

~

Sam's sister, Regina, appeared at the end of the path, calling as she approached. 'I've just been talking to Annie. She said Miriam is welcome to stay at the Roadhouse while you're gone.'

Sam knew Regina was fishing. He wondered how much of Jimmy's talk she'd overheard 'It's okay, sis. I told you, Miriam's cousins are coming tomorrow to keep her company.'

She stopped in front of her brother, her expression combative. 'Well, alright then. But you know Tau has plenty of questions about the man with the funny voice in the big metal thingie.' She paused, raising an eyebrow. 'As a matter of fact, so do I.'

'Where is that nephew of mine hiding?' asked Sam, clearly eager to change the subject.

Regina folded her arms, her lips compressed into a stubborn line. He wondered if they were about to have another interminable stand-off. He glanced at Mallory, but she was still staring at the top of the gorge, and he imagined her still trying to track the long-gone helicopter across the empty sky.

He looked back to his sister, his tone placatory. 'Come on, it's police business, sis. You and Tau should get packed if you're leaving for Annie's today.'

Regina sighed and dropped her arms by her side. 'Alright. I'll text you when I get there.' She walked up to him, gave him a soft fist bump, glanced at Mallory and said, 'Take care of yourself, Miriam.'

~

Silence settled between them after Regina disappeared into the house. Mallory sat down on the bench near the spring, watching shadows lengthen across the lower reaches of the gorge. She closed her eyes for a moment and enjoyed the cooling effect of dusk. When she opened them, she glanced up at Sam who stood beside her, observing the last rays playing across the rock wall of the gorge. She followed the wall upwards, measuring the distance from the ground to the first ledge with a practised eye, her gaze continuing to follow the ledge to an open fissure in the rocks approximately halfway up the wall.

Sam sat down beside her. 'I love dusk out here. The deep sunsets, the softness in the air. There's as much promise in the coming night as there is in the dawn.'

Mallory smiled. 'Careful now, you're starting to sound like a hopeless romantic. Next minute, you'll be reciting poetry.'

He smiled, his green eyes dancing. 'Don't tempt me. If anything could make me recite poetry, this country could.'

Mallory felt her breath catch for a moment when he

smiled. He looked so relaxed and happy. She was reminded of their first kiss a lifetime ago, before she had to hide from the world, before she realised that he was a cop. She wanted to reach out and touch him for a moment, but residual anger at his recent manipulation kept her still. It was hard to believe he could lie to her so easily. Sam put his finger to his lips and pointed halfway up the gorge wall. A mob of yellow-footed rock wallabies sat on the ledge, studying the humans on the bench below them.

'They're endangered now,' Sam whispered. 'It's so good to see them here.'

'Sam!' Regina's voice startled the wallabies. Mallory watched enviously as they scattered up the wall of the gorge in easy bounds. 'We're heading off now,' Regina called.

Sam stood up and stretched. 'We'll say goodbye to Tau.'

The pair walked around the side of the house to Regina's four-wheel drive. Tau ran toward Sam with his arms outstretched.

Sam scooped him up. 'Goodbye, little man. Be good for Mumma, and keep a lookout for old man roo on the road.'

'Sure Uncy.' The four-year-old threw his arms around Sam's neck. 'I'll miss you, Uncy.'

Sam squeezed him gently. 'I'll be back soon.'

Tau grinned at Mallory over Sam's shoulder. 'Goodbye, Miss Miriam.'

Mallory leant in and kissed the boy. He pulled a face and scrubbed at his cheek with a chubby fist. She laughed. 'You're a cheeky one, Tau.'

He grinned again. 'When are you and Uncy getting married?'

Mallory's cheeks burned. 'Wha–what gave you that idea?' she stammered.

'Mumma told Aunty Annie that she would put money on—'

'Tau!' Regina moved quickly, lifting the boy out of Sam's arms. She avoided looking at her brother as she marched Tau toward the Landcruiser. 'He's confused,' she muttered.

The boy jumped up and down on the spot in offended rage. 'That's not true, Mumma, you said—'

'We have to go now, my little roo spotter,' Regina interrupted. She lifted him up and popped him into the car, slamming the door on his protests.

Sam grinned without embarrassment while Mallory went a deeper shade of red at his sister's transparent attempt to hush Tau. She felt a stab of envy as Regina leapt into the vehicle and gunned the engine. If only she could get away that easily. With Jimmy on the loose, the best place for everyone was anywhere but this gorge.

Sam and Mallory watched the four-wheel drive disappear into the expanse beyond the gorge. She scraped the dust back and forth with her boot, suddenly self-conscious around him after Tau's outburst.

Sam cleared his throat to get her attention and frowned into the gathering darkness. 'I need to call the super. Jimmy turning up here will change what happens tomorrow.'

Mallory didn't trust herself to speak. She was angry, and a plan was already formulating. She needed Sam out of the picture if she had any hope of making it work, but part of her didn't want him to leave either.

He smiled. 'I'll get this call out of the way, and then we'll get dinner on, yeah?'

She avoided his gaze and nodded, glad to be back on neutral ground.

~

By the time Sam finished talking on the phone, the night had claimed the last of the sunset. The glow of the solar-powered lights softened the lines of the kitchen, causing the burnished redwood benchtops to gleam. He stepped into the room, enjoying the sound of classical music floating amongst rustic shelves, gilded plates, wicker baskets and metal beakers stuffed with wildflowers and eucalypt on the sideboard.

Sam hated to break the mood, but he wanted to reassure Mallory that the situation with Jimmy was in hand.

'The super has changed your handlers.' He moved to the sink and started pulling a head of lettuce apart, dropping the leaves into a bowl. He glanced up and caught her reflection on the window as she moved around the table, placing cutlery and lighting candles. 'He said they're from Sydney. I've never met them, but they sound like they'll be a good fit for you.'

Mallory continued to move around the table without acknowledging him.

He dropped his eyes, concentrating on washing the salad. 'They're senior operatives. We can't take chances with Jimmy on the loose.' He looked up again, watching her red sundress ripple in the mirrored reflection, the effect making her appear to glide across the floor.

She looked at the window, and he dropped his eyes. When he looked up again, she was standing beside him.

'Can I help with anything?'

She was so close he could feel her breath on his neck. A wave of unexpected desire passed through his body, and he shook the greens with more force than necessary. Water splashed onto Mallory's dress, making her laugh. 'Wow, you could just say no.'

He dropped the greens in the sink, turned and looked in her eyes. She stopped laughing and swayed toward him. He was reminded of the first time they met in the desert, and the night he had tracked her to her motel in Coober Pedy. Before he could think about what he was doing, he cupped her face in his hands and kissed her. He felt the thrill of touching her run through his body and didn't want the moment to end. He drew her closer as the kiss deepened.

Sam felt Mallory's initial surprise at the kiss turn quickly into desire. His fingers burned into the skin of her cheek, and she sighed and pressed into him. When he put an arm around her waist and pulled her closer, she ran her hands up his neck into his hair, and all thoughts of the present and future were suspended as they both sunk further into the kiss.

A sudden hammering at the door made them spring apart. 'Walker!'

'Bloody coppers and the way they knock,' Mallory muttered.

He stared at her, his expression dazed. 'They weren't supposed to be here until tomorrow.'

He strode to the door, aware that he and Mallory would have been visible through the window to the pair waiting outside. He stood to the side as the two female operatives entered the room.

The taller of the two gave a mock salute and held out her ID. 'Mowbray, at your service.'

Sam frowned at her tone, and her smile dropped away. 'Why the long face, Walker?'

'I've just been on the phone to the super. You weren't supposed to get here tonight,' he said.

Mowbray glanced at her partner and Sam wondered at her expression, but before he could consider it further, she turned back to him and raised an eyebrow. 'We made good time, and I'm sure you're both relieved we've turned up. Although it appears you were handling things just fine when we arrived.'

Sam's face went a deep shade of red as he returned to the sink, grabbed the salad and tossed the leaves into a bowl. He glanced at Mallory, but she refused to meet his gaze.

She turned her back on him and opened the fridge, offering the women drinks. 'Have you had dinner?' she asked.

Mowbray leaned against a bench with her arms folded across her ribs. 'We've eaten, thanks.' She glanced at her companion again. 'What do you say, Hodges?' She smirked. 'Let's get settled in and let these two finish preparing their *dinner*.'

Hodges nodded. 'We'll need a debrief afterwards, Walker.'

Mallory and Sam giggled like children after the women left the room. He held up a hand, hushing her before they became too loud. 'I'm going to be in enough trouble because of that, you know, and rightly so. They shouldn't have been able to get to the door undetected.'

'Sorry.'

'Not your fault. I'm the one on duty.' He gestured toward the table. 'Let's eat. I have an early start tomorrow.'

The pair started dinner, but there was an awkwardness that had not been present before the women arrived. Their earlier passion caused them to both speak at once, stumble over words, then stop in embarrassment.

~

The tension filled the pauses in their conversation until Mallory felt she could take no more. She excused herself and fled to her room. It disturbed her, the way Sam could make her forget herself, the way he could play her body like an instrument and then act as if nothing had happened. She shuddered at the memory of his fingers brushing against the skin on the back of her arms and tried to get her thoughts under control. She picked up her hairbrush and dragged it through her curls, reminding herself that he was a copper, that he'd already proven more than once that he was prepared to choose the law over her.

She dropped the brush and threw herself onto her bed, staring at the gauze curtains floating back and forth in the breeze from the open window. Jimmy's appearance at the gorge and the information he'd brought returned to her. She tried to stop the wide smile stretching across her face, but eventually gave in to it. Her father was out there somewhere! She was sure of it, now. It seemed that she could almost feel his presence near her. After so many years of uncertainty, there was finally proof that he was alive! She didn't believe for one moment that someone else was wearing the Topaz Stallion on their pinkie. Her father was alive and in danger.

She hadn't waited most of her life for a sign that he was

alive just to lose him before she could find him. She didn't care what Sam thought, or how her actions made him feel. While Jimmy the Cat was on the loose hunting her father, she had no intention of playing it safe, and remaining in hiding in the middle of the Australian outback.

~

Mallory woke, disoriented in the complete darkness of the room. The sound of raised voices drifted along the hall from the kitchen. Her eyes adjusted to the lack of light and she looked at her watch. 12:30am. She regulated her breathing and strained to hear what was being said, but could only hear the low rumble of Sam's voice and a sentence here or there from the women. She rolled her eyes, catching Hodges' words, 'too invested' and 'informing the super first thing'.

It was another hour before silence settled over the house. She sat up and slipped into her clothes, every nerve tuned to the creaks and groans of metal and wood shifting in the cooling night. She opened her door a crack and glanced up and down the hall. The stillness was complete. All of the bedroom doors were closed, but she knew she'd have to be careful. Sam had a sixth sense, and even if her movements didn't wake him, he would be up and about before dawn.

She crept barefooted along the hallway, pausing in the kitchen to grab a rucksack on the table. A muffled thud from one of the bedrooms made her pause, rucksack raised in the air. If any of them caught her there, with the rucksack in her hands, the game would be up. Her heart hammered, but she stayed completely still and waited until she was sure it was safe to move. She slung the bag over her back and slipped out the door at the rear of the building.

She stopped on the veranda, picked up her trainers, turned them upside down, and knocked them as quietly as possible against the ground. Despite the soft thunking noise they made, she was unable to stop herself from performing this very Australian ritual. She paused for a moment, listening for any movement inside the house, and grinned for a second at herself, squatting there in red dust, checking for spiders in her shoes.

She slipped the trainers on, glanced up at the low-hanging moon in the sky above, and whispered a silent thank you for the crisp light it provided. She could use the torch on her phone, but there was a risk it might be seen if someone woke in the house. She jogged along the sandy path to the bottom of the gorge and started to climb.

After climbing silently for fifteen metres, she reached the ledge, and crept along its narrow edge, her feet sideways and back to the wall, until it widened into the vertical fissure. She reached inside the fissure and pulled out a pouch, and then placed the rucksack from the house on wider section of the ledge, taking care when she opened it to ensure that nothing was disturbed around the object it contained.

Mallory looked back at the house and shifted her position until a tree screened her presence on the ledge. She took a photo of the interior of the rucksack and, with the light hidden behind her body, turned on her torch. She unrolled the pouch, and smiled. The makeup and wig she'd hidden had not been compromised by months out in the weather. She wrapped them back into the soft leather folds, selected the tools she required from a separate pocket and went to work. The delicate operation required her full attention, but she kept one ear trained on the house. If she were discovered now, there would be no chance of finding her father.

An hour later, she rolled up the pouch and slid it into the back of her shorts. She checked the photo she'd taken of the rucksack against the interior, closed the zipper, and climbed down the gorge wall. As she approached the house, she was careful to keep to the trees beside the path. She stopped near the door, removed her trainers, and brushed any traces of red dust off the rucksack. Waiting beside the door for a moment, she cocked her head to one side and listened, but there was no movement inside.

Slipping into the house, she replaced the rucksack on the kitchen table where she had found it and went to the bathroom, stripping off her clothes in the dark, and pushing them into the wash basket. Then she pulled on an oversized t-shirt she'd left in the bathroom earlier and placed the pouch into her knickers. After checking for any traces of dust on her hands and face, she flushed the toilet and washed her hands. She double checked her appearance, messing up her hair and drooping her eyes as if she'd just got out of bed. She had to ensure that there was no risk that anyone who may be waiting outside in the hall would consider her actions suspicious.

She opened the door, rubbing her eyes and yawning as she made her way along the hall. When she made it back to the safety of her room, she pulled the covers up to her chin and tried to calm the adrenalin coursing through her body. It seemed unlikely she would get any sleep tonight.

~

Mallory snapped awake and stared at the soft green glow of

the numbers on the clock face. 5:30am! She jumped up and padded down the hall to the kitchen, sure that she would catch Sam before he left. When she reached the doorway, she stopped and tried to look nonchalant.

Mowbray and Hodges sat at either ends of the table, with laptops open. They looked up at her and glanced at each other.

'He's already gone,' said Mowbray.

Hodges nodded. 'We thought it preferable he get to Canberra as soon as possible.' She closed her laptop with a snap. 'We're moving you to a safe location today.'

Mallory frowned. 'Canberra? I thought he was going to Sydney?'

Hodges sneered. 'It appears you don't have the inside track after all.'

Mallory kept her tone brisk to hide her distress at the thought of Sam lying to her, 'Where are you taking me?'

Mowbray studied her for a moment, and Mallory was careful to hide the equal parts of disappointment and excitement that were suddenly at war inside her.

'You don't need to know until we get there.'

She moved to the bench, grabbed a coffee without answering and went outside, needing to put space between herself and the watchful women in the house. She sat on the bench near the spring, sipped her coffee and watched the sun's rays slowly appear over the top of the gorge. The light lit up the golds, oranges and reds on the rock face with such intensity that the rocks appeared to be burning. She smiled at the fiery display, her thoughts returning to Sam's comment the day before. It was special country and she would miss the beauty of the gorge, but there were plenty of beautiful places on earth, and she couldn't stay here anyway. Her father was out there somewhere. She had to get to him before Jimmy.

~

Mallory placed her coffee cup on the drainer and surveyed the empty kitchen. She leaned across the sink and flicked the curtain to one side. Her handlers were engrossed in conversation as they packed bags into the back of the vehicle with methodical precision. She glanced at the suitcases sitting on the ground and made a rough calculation. It wouldn't be long until her time at the gorge was history. She would be going to who-knew-where, but no doubt it would be somewhere remote. She'd have to make a loose plan and be prepared to change it, or act on any opportunity that might arise. She also had to accept that there was every chance that her plans would fail. She let the curtain drop and moved to the other side of the room. The rucksack on the table caught her eye. She forced herself to loosen up and relax. Everything that could be done had been done. It was up to her to seize the right opportunity and put her plan into action.

She moved toward the rear of the house, closing her bedroom door and peering out the window toward the gorge wall. The raucous laughter of kookaburras, as loud as a barrage of gunshots, cracked open the morning silence. A flock of black cockatoos lifted out of the trees near the wall, and Mallory paused for a second at the sight. She had a sudden vision of Sam with Tau, inspecting the lizards and bugs that resided in the rocks beside the spring. She already missed his presence, his easy smile and grace, the low rumble of his voice when he schooled Tau on the natural wonders of the land. An image returned to her, of Sam stepping out of the spring, the artesian water streaming off his shoulders and chest. She felt a flutter deep in her belly. It spread through her body, making her stomach flip and her legs tremble. She would miss his company, his laughter and his smile. The murmur of the women's voices near the front door jolted her out of her reverie. She pushed all thoughts of Sam away and returned to her room. Now was not the time for sentimentality.

A few moments later, Mowbray rapped on her door. 'Mallory! We have to sort a few things out with you before we can travel.'

Mallory frowned at the sound of her real name, and a flicker of unease flashed through her. She opened the door and followed Mowbray to the kitchen.

Hodges motioned to a chair at the end of the table. Mallory sat and looked from one officer to the other, careful to keep her expression neutral. 'Why are you using my real name?'

The pair glanced at each other. 'We'll stop once we're on the road.'

Suspicion gripped Mallory. 'What do you mean, sort a few things out?' she asked.

Hodges unzipped the rucksack on the table. 'You're still considered a flight risk.' She pulled the monitor out of the bag. 'You have to wear this while we travel.'

Mallory rolled her eyes. 'As if! Where am I going to run to out here?' She jumped up. 'Christ, I'm sure to stand out with that thing on my ankle.'

Mowbray narrowed her eyes. 'No, you won't stand out,'

she said, 'because you'll take those shorts off and wear these lovely flares.' She tossed a pair of jeans toward Mallory.

'Bit bloody hot for jeans,' Mallory muttered.

Mowbray folded her arms. 'Put them on. Better than the alternative.'

Mallory registered the threat in the woman's voice, and her suspicion increased. She sighed and dumped her bag on the table, huffing her displeasure as she removed her shorts and pulled on the jeans.

Hodges motioned to the chair again. 'Just channel your inner hippie. I'm sure you'll be fine.'

Mallory dropped onto the chair like a sulky teenager. 'Do I look like a bloody hippie?' She watched the woman lock the bracelet onto her ankle.

When Hodges finished, she looked up into Mallory's face and shook her head. 'I'm certain you can manage to look like whatever you want.' She stood up, looking down at Mallory, her contempt apparent. 'Anyway, no point taking attitude, missy. This is for your own safety.'

It took all of Mallory's self-control to stop the laughter that was bubbling up inside her. She scowled instead. 'Don't patronise me.'

Hodges scowled in return. 'Don't make it so easy, then.'

Mallory looked from one woman to the other. Their behaviour hung in perfect suspension in her mind for a second. It was worth considering further, the familiar feel of it causing a small frisson of alarm, but the thought slid away under the pressure of the situation.

She stood and stomped toward the front door. 'We may as well get going.'

The women exchanged a glance behind her before following her to the vehicle.

~

Mowbray turned in the passenger seat and smiled at Mallory as she unfolded a map. 'We're going old-school. There's no hacking into a paper map.'

Mallory tried to match the warmth of the other woman's smile, her own tentative. Since leaving the gorge, both officers seemed intent on building an atmosphere of camaraderie, as if the three of them were friends on the road-trip of a lifetime.

'Where are we headed?' She kept her tone casual as she looked out the window at the featureless landscape scudding past.

Hodges glanced in the rear-view mirror. 'It's a surprise. You'll see when we get there.'

Mallory kept her gaze on the flat, red plains outside the car. It wouldn't do to ask too many questions, and it would be easy enough to get her bearings when she needed to. Besides, they would have to stop for gas and food at some point. Thoughts of Sam came out of nowhere, and she winced at the emptiness she felt. Mallory knew that what she was going to do meant she'd never see him again. They were on the wrong side of the tracks. Her plan would ensure there'd be no going back to police protection, and no place for her in his life.

Some small, selfish part of her couldn't help holding on. Mallory remembered his touch, his kisses, and wondered what it'd be like to spend a night with him. She imagined sitting with him beside a campfire, watching the endless stars in the Australian night sky wheeling above them. She closed her eyes and let the fantasy take over – she could see Sam pulling his shirt off, the fire making his skin glow like treacle in the dark. She almost reached out, wanting to run her hands over his chest. Instead, she opened her eyes.

Mallory shook herself, forcing Sam out of her consciousness. Loss of concentration was one of the risks of long road-trips, and she had no intention of failing. She watched Mowbray's head bounce as she started to nod off. Mallory ran her eyes over the interior of the car. Her backpack was between her feet with the pouch safely inside. She knew the officers had buried her main bag beneath the rest of the luggage. She almost grinned, but kept her face impassive. She didn't need anything in the suitcase, and didn't care about the contents either.

Hodges hit a pothole and Mowbray's head jerked up. 'How far are we from the Auburn Roadhouse?'

Hodges frowned at her. 'About an hour. Why?'

'Think it's time we changed driver. We can't afford to have an accident. And I need to stretch my legs.'

They pulled over on the edge of the deserted highway, unclicking their seatbelts before the vehicle finished rolling. Mowbray stepped out of the car and walked to the driver's side, opening the door for Hodges. Mallory could feel Mowbray's gaze on her through the window as she stood beside the driver's door. There was no escaping to anywhere on this road. She remained relaxed, her head resting on the cool glass of the window. Mowbray stepped into the vehicle and gunned the engine as she continued her desultory conversation with Hodges.

Mallory was no longer listening. She had seen the Auburn Roadhouse on a map before and had a general idea of its location. Excitement gripped her stomach as the beginnings of a plan started to form.

She sunk deeper into the door, pressing her cheek against the window and closed her eyes.

After a few minutes, the conversation stuttered.

She heard Hodges whisper, 'She's finally sleeping.'

Mowbray's reply rolled into an indiscernible, low growl.

Mallory slipped her hand into the side pocket of her rucksack and grabbed the pouch. A shiver of terror at the thought of losing it ran through her as she slid it into her boot.

~

The three women climbed out of the vehicle, the stiffness of their movements giving away the length of time they'd been on the road. Mallory stretched her arms over her head, swaying her torso from side to side as she took in the area surrounding the roadhouse. A group of men lounging in the shade at the front of the roadhouse nudged each other, grinning as they openly appraised the women. Hodges surveyed the empty road and sparsely populated carpark before taking in the area around the bowsers, until her gaze finally came to rest on the group of men in the shadows.

One gave a low whistle and called out, 'Would you fine fillies like to join us for a drink?'

Hodges' shoulders stiffened, a frown settling on her brow.

Mowbray muttered, 'At ease, Miss, they're only harmless boys.'

Hodges snorted and rolled her eyes toward the sky.

Mallory watched the exchange and considered the

group of men at the front of the roadhouse. They displayed the first stages of rowdiness that came with day drinking. Their movements were loose, slightly uncoordinated, their voices and laughter loud. They could certainly be relied on to cause a distraction.

She saw a toilet sign, and an arrow pointing toward the back of the roadhouse. The word jolted her, reminding her how far she was from her home in Canada.

She tapped Mowbray on the shoulder. 'I need the restroom.' She didn't wait for an answer, slipping on sunglasses and pulling her cap down over her face as she walked across the forecourt. When she reached the restroom, she looked out the window at a few dust-covered vehicles and a row of semi-trailers in the overflow carpark behind the roadhouse. Behind the carpark was an endless backdrop of flat, empty plains. She noticed a motorbike amongst the cars. A helmet sat on the seat. There was a chance the keys might still be with the bike. The surge of excitement dissipated as quickly as it occurred. She stood for a moment, staring at her reflection in the mirror, the bleak reality of the situation assailing her. She needed time to get well away from her handlers, or they would hunt her down. There was no way she could escape on a motorbike without immediate detection in this place.

When she opened the door, Mowbray and Hodges were waiting outside. The quick, silent exchange between the women made her blood run cold. She had a sudden premonition that she was not the only one nursing an unknown agenda.

Hodges looked her up and down. 'What took you so long?'

Mallory looked at her over the top of her sunglasses. 'Do you want a blow-by-blow account?'

'Smartass,' Hodges huffed as she pushed past her and slammed the door.

Mowbray put a hand on Mallory's arm. 'Wait here until we're ready.'

'I'm not a prisoner, you know.'

'You're not a free agent, either. And believe me, you don't want to go near that lot out front on your own.'

Mallory nodded and considered the situation. The look between the women when she came out of the restroom had jolted her instinct into overdrive. There were already enough reasons to want to be free of them, but that look had just given her another. She knew the young men near the front could be relied on to cause a distraction, but the roadhouse was otherwise deserted. Even if she managed to have enough time to get into disguise, it would take a miracle to get away from those two bulldogs in the restroom. She stared at the expanse of glass surrounding the interior of the roadhouse. Once inside, the women would be able to see all vehicles arriving and leaving the roadhouse.

A Greyhound bus pulled into the Roadhouse carpark, sending a gritty pall of dust over the three women as they made their way to the front of the building. Mallory glanced over her shoulder and watched wave after wave of grey-haired couples and scantily-clad backpackers pour from the bus. She turned away, careful to hide her interest from the women flanking her. One of the men at the front of the service station jumped up, bowing to the three women as the automatic doors shuddered open and released a blast of icy air from inside.

'Ethan at your service! To be sure, you're welcome at the Auburn Roadhouse, ladies. Will you be dining at this fine establishment today?' he asked.

Mallory grinned at his accent, and wanted to ask how an Irishman managed the heat in outback Australia, but Mowbray grabbed her by the arm and hissed in her ear, 'Jesus, you're not flirting with the riff-raff. Are you trying to draw attention?'

The doors closed on the men, but Mallory felt them watching with interest when she pulled her arm free. 'I think you're doing a good enough job for both of us.'

Laughter broke out in the group of men outside the door.

One of the young men yelled, 'Wasting your time, Ethan old mate. Looks like they're batting for the opposition.' A wave of laughter swelled through the group, ending in whistles as two young women from the bus approached the door.

Hodges stepped inside and glared at the menu behind the counter. 'Let's just get food and get out of here.'

After they ordered, the women sat at a table in the corner where Hodges and Mowbray could observe people coming and going. Mallory watched a truck driver walk toward his rig and unlock the front cabin. He rolled the window down and disappeared inside for a moment before jumping down and moving toward the trailer to check the load. A young woman wearing jeans and a t-shirt similar to her own left the restaurant and walked toward the toilets, blocking Mallory's view of the truck for a moment.

Mallory placed her burger on the table. 'I don't feel so good. I need to go back to the restroom.'

Hodges and Mowbray stared at their chips and burgers, before glaring at Mallory.

She nodded toward the window. 'You can see all the way to the restrooms from here. I won't be long.' She pulled a face, said, 'I think I'm going to throw up,' and jumped up before they could argue, bolting for the front door.

When she reached the restroom, she smiled at the closed cubicle door, locked the outside door, and ran water while she waited.

The young woman came out of the cubicle and smiled at Mallory. 'Hey, I saw you at the next table. You guys aren't on the bus,' she said.

'No.' Mallory stretched up and peered out the slits between the louvres near the door. 'I'm here with a couple of my workmates. Did you see them?'

The girl nodded and turned on the tap.

'Yeah, we're supposed to be filming the "real outback", but jeez they're a pair of basic bitches.' Mallory rolled her eyes and grinned.

The girl smiled uncertainly as she finished washing her hands. 'They did look a bit uptight.'

Mallory grinned and thrust out her hand. 'They sure are! I'm Mandy. What's your name?'

The girl smiled again. 'Sarah. I'm traveling to the Northern Territory. I have a job on a station up there.'

Mallory stared at her wide-eyed. 'Wow. That sounds amazing!' She spread her arms. 'Are you going to fly choppers, ride horses, fight buffalo?'

The other girl laughed. 'God, no. I'm a governess.'

'Well kids are scarier than flying choppers and fighting

buffalo,' Mallory laughed.

Sarah joined in, her eyes dancing. 'You know, you're right about that, for sure.'

'Hey,' Mallory leant close to the girl, her tone conspiratorial, 'Do you want to have some fun? Play a joke on the boring old cows I work with?'

Sarah shrugged. 'Depends.'

'You see, they won't let me out of their sight. Clocking every damn minute, reporting me to the bosses back in Sydney for every little thing. They're sticklers for time and motion.' Mallory rubbed her chin. 'I probably won't have a job when I get back to Sydney. I just want some time out, yeah? I've been stuck with them for three days solid.' She winked. 'Now, they're complaining because I had a little flirt with the guys at the door.'

Sarah's eyes widened.

'Hey, would you mind terribly causing a distraction?' Mallory continued.

Sarah looked uncertain.

'Just throw on my cap and sunnies, and chat to the guys at the front there. Just to wind those cows up again.'

Sarah pulled a face, her hesitation obvious.

Mallory winked. 'Oh, come on, those fellas are harmless. I just want a moment to myself for a quick ciggie, then I'll be right behind you.'

The girl giggled. 'Okay! I promised my mum I would have an adventure in Australia. I guess this qualifies.'

Mallory handed her cap and sunglasses to the girl before slipping into the empty cubicle. She pulled the pouch out of the bracelet on her ankle and worked quickly to release the locking mechanism that she had disabled at the gorge. Then she grabbed the wig and makeup kit and went to work.

On the other side of the door, the girl cleared her throat. 'So, should I wait for you?'

'Nah, you go for it,' Mallory said. 'I'll be right behind you after I finish my smoke. You won't have to deal with my workmates. They'll be too busy frying my butt to worry about you.'

When Sarah left the restroom, Mallory applied the finishing touches to her disguise, and waited for the young men to acknowledge Sarah's presence near the front of the roadhouse. As soon as the wolf-whistles started, she flicked the slats on the front window and watched the crowd at the door shift and block the view to the toilets. She slipped outside and darted along the side of the building, then angled toward the idling truck in the carpark. The driver was moving along the far side of the truck, his legs visible from the other side. She crossed her fingers and ran toward the driver's door.

Before she climbed up the side of the truck, she glanced at the empty carpark, then dove through the open window, scrambling into the sleeping bay behind the driver's seat. Adrenaline surged through her body, making her head pound and her chest contract. She took a deep breath, concentrating on bringing her shaking hands under control. She looked around for a hiding place, aware that she didn't have much time, before moving to the back of the sleeping cabin and sliding into the gap between the mattress and wall, working her body down to the bottom until she was pressed against the hot, rutted metal of the cab floor.

She heard the driver whistling as he approached the cab.

He opened the door and she held her breath as he wound up the window, jumped onto the ground outside and locked the truck. She let out her breath with a gasp as he walked away, and started to regulate her breathing, counting until it was light and silent and finally drowned by the commotion she expected that was erupting near the roadhouse.

2

SAM strode into the Canberra office, intent on reaching his desk before the superintendent noticed his return. He took the back corridors, skirting around the main cluster of offices.

He was opening the door to his office when he heard the super bellow, 'Walker! What are you doing here?'

He turned around, his heart sinking, his hopes of a quiet and painless entry dashed. Everyone in the office paused. There were no murmuring voices, no click of fingers on keyboards. The silence made him feel exposed as the rest of the team watched him head toward the super's office.

He closed the door behind him and waited for the super to acknowledge his presence.

The other man sighed and closed a file, dropping it on top of a stack to the right of him, before gesturing at a seat on the other side of the desk. 'Sit.'

Sam slid into the chair, his stomach twisting in anxiety as he waited.

'Are you less than happy to see me, Walker?'

Sam stared at the super in alarm. 'I don't understand, Sir.'

'You roll in here after six months away,' the super's nails tapped rhythmically on the desk, sending Sam's nerves into freefall, 'With no explanation about your unexpected presence in this office. And no hugs, no questions about my life? Not even a simple hello?'

Sam's stomach tightened further when the super leaned back into his chair and smiled. It felt like playing bluff with an angry bear.

'Unexpected presence? Hugs, Sir?'

The super laughed, but there was very little humour in the sound. 'Perhaps a hug was stretching the joke a bit, Walker.'

Sam relaxed slightly. 'I wanted to get on with my report, Sir.'

The super's smile widened. 'As it happens, I've had a comprehensive report, Walker.'

Sam's gut clenched tighter than he thought was possible, and a wave of heat rose up his neck and into his cheeks. Mowbray and Hodges had filled the super in on his lapse.

The other man frowned at him. 'You good, Walker? You don't seem yourself.'

'Just tired, Sir.'

The super raised an eyebrow and flicked open the file in front of him. 'We're certain Jimmy Contanti has already left the country,' he said. 'At least we don't have to play host to Interpol and God knows who else.'

He retrieved the file from the stack and held it toward Sam. 'Take a look at the MO on Warwick Cash.' He shook his head. 'Everyone always says he's a gentleman robber and an all-round good guy. That file says otherwise.'

Sam couldn't concentrate on the file. The super's behaviour didn't make sense. If he'd been briefed by Mowbray and Hodges, surely he would have gone on the attack. He wondered if the super was toying with him, but the scenario seemed unlikely. He knew he could expect immediate accountability for any mistakes. He leant forward, ready to ask about the Mowbray and Hodges report, but a knock on the door stopped him.

The super frowned at the closed door. 'Come in!'

The door swung open and the super grinned mirthlessly. 'Ah, Clementine. To what do we owe the honour?'

The young man stopped, his body turned awkwardly toward the hall, his face reddening. 'I've some strange data, Sir.' He glanced at Sam, but looked away just as quickly when he nodded at him.

The super drummed his fingers on the desk. 'Is there something to report?'

'I'm not sure, Sir.'

'Then why are you here?'

Clementine cleared his throat nervously, and glanced at Sam again. 'Well—'

'Spit it out, man!'

'It's Mowbray and Hodges, Sir.' Sweat popped out on the younger man's forehead and his face went a deeper shade of red as beads started to swell and roll down his temples. Sam felt a pang of sympathy for him. He understood how nerve-wracking it could be, having to face the super with bad news. He placed the file on the desk, and decided he should be the one to broach the subject of the two operatives with Mallory.

He leant forward and looked the super in the eye. 'Did Mowbray and Hodges send you a debrief?'

'That's expecting a bit much, Walker, considering they would have passed you on the way out the door this morning.'

Clementine cleared his throat and ran an exploratory finger between his dampened collar and neck. He pulled irritably at his tie before turning to the super. 'I've been trying to contact them all morning, Sir, to see when they expect to arrive. They're not signing in.'

'What?' Sam felt like he'd been punched in the gut. 'They arrived last night!'

Alarm spread across the super's face. 'But that's not possible! I sent copies of their ID and the run sheet last night via the usual channel. Did you receive that?'

Sam shook his head, his alarm growing. 'They arrived last night. Said they'd made good time. They showed me their ID and run sheets last night. That's why I'm here instead of Sydney!'

The super grabbed his mobile and dialled a number, drumming his fingers while he waited for an answer. He glanced at Sam. 'I'll try Hodges.' He dialled again and waited. After a few moments, he stood up and punched a new number into the phone. After what seemed an eternity, he said, 'We have a problem with Operation Topaz.' He turned back to Sam and dropped his phone on the desk. 'We need to get down to the operations centre, pronto. Full descriptions and anything else that may be pertinent. I don't think I need to tell you Mallory Cash has been compromised.'

~

Sam paced in front of the bank of monitors while information on the women posing as Mowbray and Hodges was entered into the computer. He could barely keep his patience in check as he ran over the details he'd given to the super. He wanted to be sure that he hadn't missed anything, no matter how minor it may seem. He stopped pacing when identikit photos of the women appeared on one of the screens. Their likenesses were good, and he hoped they would find matches in the database.

The super appeared beside him, leant toward him and whispered, 'We've found Mowbray and Hodges.'

Sam raised an eyebrow. The older man put a hand on his arm and tipped his head toward an office door. 'We need to talk.'

Sam followed the super, his heart hammering. He knew without asking that Mallory was in serious danger.

The super closed the door. When he turned to Sam, his face was drawn and pale and a pulse jumped on his temple. 'Mowbray and Hodges were found in a dumpster on the outskirts of Adelaide.' His voice caught and he stopped to run a shaking hand through his hair. 'I know you never met them, but Mowbray and Hodges were staunch. Two of our best.' He dropped his head for a moment and then slammed a hand onto the desk. 'We had no reason to suspect she was in immediate danger!' He slumped into his chair and shook his head. 'I blame myself. I should have put extra security measures in place after Jimmy Contanti's visit.'

Sam folded his arms across his chest and concentrated on keeping his breathing steady. Every nerve in his body screamed and his skin felt like it was on fire. He pressed his hands into his armpits, clenching his fists against the adrenaline rushing through his body. He wondered if this was how it felt to lose control. 'Has anyone heard anything?'

The super shook his head. 'We've put an alert out with the police up north, and we already have operatives on the ground in South Australia. We're being discreet for obvious reasons, but it's being shared through plenty of channels now. I don't believe they can get too far out there without detection.' He frowned. 'I just hope they're taking her somewhere because we both know the alternative isn't good.' He pulled a file out of a stack on the side of his desk and pushed it towards him. 'Best to stay positive and focus on bringing her back alive. Refresh your memory on Trafford. At this point, we're sure Contanti led two of Trafford's people to Mallory.'

~

Mallory stayed completely still inside the truck, pressing deeper into her hiding spot at the sound of running feet approaching. She took a deep breath to stave off the panic that threatened to engulf her and kept her attention on the sounds outside the truck. Fists started to hammer on a vehicle outside, and she heard the distinctive whoosh of bus doors opening.

'What's going on out here?' yelled the bus driver.

'We're police officers. We need to search the bus.'

Mallory winced at the growl in Mowbray's voice, and hoped the bus driver would cooperate. A period of silence followed. Mallory started to overheat in the locked cabin, and resisted the urge to wipe at the sweat rolling down her face and neck.

She heard the women's boots hit the gravel as they jumped back out of the bus, and the whoosh of the doors shutting. The crunch of boots on gravel and muttering female voices came closer to the truck. The sudden flick and clunk of someone trying the handle made her breath catch and stop.

A thump sounded on the lower part of the door, followed by another louder thump.

'Oi! What ya doing, hitting my truck?'

Mallory almost jumped at the sound of the truck driver's voice. She stared into the darkness under the mattress and tried to control the cramping panic that had rushed through her body when she heard the man speak. If the women flashed their badges and insisted he open the cab, they would find her. She wasn't sure what their agenda was, but she wasn't prepared to put her life on it falling in her favour.

She heard Mowbray speak and strained to hear her reply, caught the words 'dangerous fugitive' and rolled her eyes.

'Yeah, well there's no need to punch my truck because you can't do ya job, lady. I'll send the government a bloody bill if there's a dent.'

'Just open the cab,' barked Hodges.

'I am gonna open the cab, and then I'm driving away. This truck has been locked all morning. Your man might be bloody dangerous, but I'll put a fiver each way that he's not Houdini.'

Mallory heard Mowbray mutter, and the truck driver laughed.

'So, a girl got the better of you, and you're throwing threats around? Lady, there's at least three people in that Roadhouse filming your bullshit right now.'

A deep silence ensued. Mallory's chest tightened with every second that passed. She wondered whether the women were weighing their options – perhaps they would use force and insist he opened the cab. She hoped the risk of being filmed was enough to deter them.

'Unless you got a warrant, you're not getting in my rig,' said the truck driver.

Mallory heard a key slide into the door, and winced. She sneaked a glance, and saw the driver's face reflected in the opposite window. He whistled as he locked the cab doors and waved at the women outside the truck, before turning the motor over and fiddling with his mirrors and seat.

As he revved the truck and started to move, he blasted the airhorns.

'That made them uptight ladies dance!' He slapped his thigh and bellowed with laughter.

Cool air seeped into the sleeping area behind the cabin and drifted across Mallory's overheated skin. She felt a wave of gratitude for the air-conditioning, relieved that they were leaving the women behind. The roar of the engine settled as the truck reached cruising speed and her eyes grew heavy under the influence of the swaying movement of the rig and the thrum of country music. She vaguely registered the volume of the music dropping, but when the driver spoke, she was jerked back into consciousness.

'You don't seem too dangerous to me, missy.'

She lifted her head up over the edge of the mattress and stared at the driver's reflection in the passenger window. He was still facing the road.

'The name's David. Nobody gets near my truck unless I let them.' He turned and stared into the rear-view mirror.

'You are no exception, young lady.'

Mallory shifted so that her eyes met his.

He smiled and nodded toward the passenger seat. 'We've been on the road three hours. I reckon you're safe to come out now.'

The floor of the sleeping cab was pressing into every bone, but Mallory still hesitated.

He smiled again. 'I can see for miles, love. They can't get the drop on us out here.'

She shimmied out of her hiding place, aware that her limbs had stiffened from remaining in one place for so long. She stretched and hopped across the console into the passenger seat.

'My name is Miriam. Why didn't you shop me?'

He smiled. 'Well, the bush telegraph's been busy out here since I hit the road this morning.'

She raised an eyebrow. 'Do tell.'

'Let's just say word is out to that there may be a young woman tangled up with some people who are not what they seem – some real nasty types. It was said that the young woman may be in need of assistance.' He glanced at her. 'You looked like you fit the scene.'

He opened the centre console and held out a Coke. 'You thirsty?'

She nodded her thanks, then realised she was thirsty and hungry.

As if reading her mind, he pulled out a box of packed sandwiches. 'Help yourself.'

They travelled in companionable silence, but Mallory's mind was racing, boiling with the words, "people who are not what they seem". She knew her instinct had been correct, and the fact that Sam hadn't realised the women were not coppers worried her. If they could trick him, they had to be serious professionals. She had no doubt that the only reason they hadn't forced their way into the truck was the risk of an uncertain outcome. A roadhouse full of tourists with rolling cameras, feisty backpackers. and hardened outback types was not the ideal place to draw attention. They knew there would be no hope of finding her again if they got it wrong. Their actions told her they were prepared to back their skills, rather than go in with guns blazing, which meant they had to be working for either Trafford or Eve, although it was most likely Trafford. Eve liked to work alone. A shudder passed through her. The scenario wasn't pleasant to think about, because she knew the women wouldn't give up. She looked out the window at the endless brown nothingness flowing past the truck and was struck by a new worry.

'Where are you headed?' she asked.

'Sydney.'

Relief coursed through her. She would find what she needed in Sydney. 'How long?'

He laughed. 'You sick of my company already, love?'

She smiled and shook her head.

'Well too bad for you if you are. You've got another eighteen hours with breaks before we get there.' He twisted his wrist and glanced at his watch. 'We'll be in Mildura before too long, though. You can stretch your legs.' He looked at her over the top of his sunglasses. 'But no running off on me if you know what's good for you.'

She stared at him, her eyes wide. 'Where would I go?'

He laughed again. 'Don't play the innocent – you seem

pretty resourceful to me. I'm sure you'd figure something out, but believe me, you're probably safer with me than on your own at the moment.'

She glanced in the mirror. Trafford's hunters were out there somewhere. No doubt already on her trail and prepared to bring her back at any cost. After all, they knew what was waiting for them if they returned without her – everyone knew what was waiting for them if they disappointed Trafford. She shuddered and craned her neck so she could see further down the road behind the truck.

'Hey.' The driver tapped his nose with an index finger. 'Don't worry. They're not going to catch up with us.'

She frowned at him and stared into the mirror again, her doubt obvious.

'You see, a couple of the fellas had serious mechanical issues a bit of a ways back.' He lifted his hands off the steering wheel, his hands scissoring together for a second. 'Do you know how hard it can be to move a road train? They've kinda blocked the road, eh.'

'Why?'

He tapped his nose again. 'The powers that be work in mysterious ways out here.'

Mallory felt her anxiety lessen. The longer the women were held up, the more chance she had of escaping detection in Sydney. She thought about her connections – if they were still prepared to help her, she could get a new passport, get out of the country and hopefully find Jimmy before the hunters found her... if the Gods were smiling.

She crossed her fingers. 'How long do you think they'll be stuck there?'

He chuckled. 'Well, I reckon you would be better off

asking how long is a piece of string, love. There's no way those trucks will move until the drivers give the nod. And there's no reception for love or money where they are now, so they can't call for backup.' He paused and geared down as they approached a deserted intersection. 'Don't worry. They're not going anywhere, or contacting anyone.'

She studied him while he manoeuvred the truck across the intersection and was tempted to ask why he was helping, but her time in outback Australia had taught her that most people didn't ask or answer questions unless completely necessary. People kept information to themselves out here, and maintained a unique sense of natural justice, making their own rules accordingly. They would defend anyone who seemed to be the underdog and worry about questions later.

When they reached the outskirts of Mildura, Mallory crawled into the sleeping cab and pulled the curtains across. David geared down as he approached a service station, and said, 'Don't worry, love, I'll park near the toilets.'

Mallory winced at the word. It didn't matter how long she stayed in Australia, it seemed strange to call restrooms by that name. She peeked between the curtains. The forecourt was deserted and the interior of the service station seemed completely devoid of life. Offers of bottomless coffee were painted across the window of the restaurant. She felt a sudden longing for a coffee from Tim Hortons. Vague nostalgia brought on a wave of memories – walking to school as the summer days began to wane, the air already crisp with impending winter, and the waft of coffee and baked goods floating out of Timmy's restarting the hunger cramping her stomach. She frowned at the unexpected memory of hunger, wanting to examine it more closely to see if it were false, but the truck shuddered to a halt, bringing her back to her present situation.

David turned to look at her. 'It'd be a good idea to keep out of sight.'

A spurt of suspicion shot through Mallory. She wondered if she should put her trust in a truck driver she'd just met, who seemed to know too much about her and the women pursuing her.

He shook his head, reading her thoughts again. 'There's something funny going on, for sure. I don't need any trouble, is all. I have my own family to think about.' He nodded toward the passenger door. 'Now go stretch your legs, powder your nose and stay outta sight.'

Mallory jumped down, the impact jarring through her stiff muscles. She kicked her legs out, shaking her arms while she stretched her neck from side to side, waiting for her muscles to uncoil. When she entered the restroom, she locked the door and stared at her reflection in the mirror before pulling out her pouch and retouching her makeup.

She thought of Sam and wondered if he knew she was in danger. Anger flared within her, and she pushed the image of his easy smile and green eyes out of her mind. She didn't need help from anyone, least of all a lawman who couldn't read a double threat when it was standing in front of him. He wouldn't hesitate to take her back in, and she would be in more danger than if she were on her own. She knew the law could not protect her from Trafford or Eve. Best to get to Sydney and leave this ridiculous country and Sam far behind. She stared blindly into the mirror, wishing she had never heard of the Virgin Rainbow, never taken the job with Trafford. She would be safe in her home in the Rockies with no one to miss and nowhere to be. She shook her head to dislodge the dark thoughts that threatened to engulf her. There was no point dwelling on the past; the only way out was forward.

When she stepped outside, the dusk air, so humid and warm after the air-conditioned cab, and the sounds of parrots squabbling and wheeling above the trees in the park opposite the station were welcome distractions. She closed her eyes, enjoying standing still in the encroaching darkness, and failed to notice a police car pull into the forecourt.

'You okay there, miss? You look a bit lost.'

Mallory's eyes snapped open, but she made her body go still and kept her expression neutral. The police officer was young, probably bored, but there could be an APB circulating. She knew that it would mention the possibility of disguise.

She smiled. 'No, just stretching my legs.'

'Oh? You don't sound local. How long have you been on the road?'

She noticed the change in his tone and was relieved to see David walking quickly toward them.

'Hey,' he said as he drew level. 'Is everything okay? Because we need to get back on the road.'

The police officer smiled. 'Where are you headed?'

'Sydney.'

The officer glanced at Mallory. 'Are you headed that way too?'

She nodded. There was no doubt in her mind the officer was fishing. The pulse in her neck started to pound, but she kept her breathing steady.

He turned away from her, as if his interest in her was done. 'I guess grabbing a passenger on the way breaks the monotony?'

David shook his head. 'No hitchers in my rig, old mate. This is my niece.'

The officer held David's gaze for a long moment before nodding. 'Taking her home to the family?' He flicked a glance at Mallory as he spoke.

David nodded. 'Is there a problem, officer?'

The other man looked at Mallory again and smiled. 'Of course not. Have a safe trip.' He turned away, glancing back at her one last time as he walked to his car.

Mallory and David strolled toward the truck without speaking. They kept their pace steady and climbed into the cab without haste. As they rolled past the police car, she glanced down and saw him talking on a cell phone. A tingle of apprehension ran down her spine when his eyes met hers.

She turned to David. 'Why did you tell the copper I was your niece?'

He shrugged and looked away, keeping his eyes on the road. 'Ah well, the law is a slow and dangerous beast, and I've never been a fan of coppers. Old habits die hard, I guess.'

She wondered again at his agenda, but his attitude was somewhat disinterested and mildly protective. There was nothing to suggest she wasn't safe. All the same, she wondered if she were doing the right thing, putting her trust in him.

~

Sam pushed through the airport crowd in the Sydney terminal, scanning for the operative he was meeting. He tried to focus, but his mind kept returning to Mallory, and he felt the low-grade knot of anxiety in the pit of his stomach tighten. There had been no sighting of her, or of the women Trafford sent since the commotion at the Auburn Roadhouse. All three had disappeared into the centre of Australia, and there was nothing coming through on the bush telegraph. The silence was unusual. The knot in his stomach tightened at the thought of Mallory alone in the desert with two killers, or worse, already dead and dumped. There was every chance she would never be found out there. He found the baggage carousel and watched the endlessly circling bags. There was no point thinking the worst. Better to keep working toward the idea that Mallory was alive and would use her skills to keep herself that way. He slipped through the bunching crowd at the edges of the carousel and hauled his backpack off the belt.

As he stepped back, someone coughed near his ear, and he felt a light touch on his elbow.

'Excuse me, Sir. Weiland, Sir.' The young man towered over him and stooped slightly as he held out his hand.

Sam looked up into his colourless eyes, taking in the nondescript grey suit, slicked-down sandy hair and old-fashioned horn-rimmed glasses. He reminded Sam of a giant, uncoordinated stick insect. He frowned at the hand, his thoughts still with Mallory. It took a moment to realise he was looking at his Sydney contact.

Weiland waited, his hand hanging in mid-air before withdrawing it. 'We don't have much time to debrief, Sir.'

Sam flushed slightly, resisting the urge to explain his rudeness to the young man. Instead, he nodded and followed him toward the terminal exit, aware that he would have to set his mind to the task of tracking Jimmy the Cat.

Weiland filled him in on the investigation as the car crawled through congested traffic. The information caused a heavy feeling of dread to settle on Sam. None of the women had been sighted; there was no new information. He felt his mind reaching out to his home country in vain hope that he would somehow feel a connection there, some reassurance that Mallory was still alive, but nothing answered. A silent emptiness filled him, as vast and as terrible as he knew the country he loved could be to people who were unfamiliar to it. He pulled his mind away, staring out the window of the car, letting the stacked buildings that hemmed the sky into knowable space take his mind off the exhaustion that threatened to consume him.

When they reached the office, he turned his thoughts toward the buzzing activity inside. He had to put Mallory's current situation out of his mind if he had any hope of helping her. He must concentrate on uncovering the smallest details around Jimmy the Cat's movements.

A stocky man threaded through the operatives. 'Walker! I'm Jock Newman. Let's get you up to speed. We've had some interesting developments in Brussels.'

Sam shook the older man's hand and tried to hide his confusion. He couldn't see what Brussels had to do with Mallory.

Newman led him to a board at the end of the office and pointed to a map. 'Trafford is on the move. Contanti is currently in France. We're waiting to see if they intend to connect.'

Sam shook his head. 'They won't be working together.'

The other man raised an eyebrow. 'You seem awful sure

of yourself.'

'It's not Jimmy the Cat's style – he hasn't worked with anyone since he did time as a young man. Whatever is going on between him and Warwick Cash seems to centre around the Topaz Stallion.' He frowned at the map. 'And it's personal.'

Newman picked up a file and flicked it open. 'Well, Walker, it would appear you're close to right. It does seem to have something to do with that bungled robbery in France over thirty years ago.' He handed the file to Sam. 'The word has always been that Contanti and his brother did the job, and Jimmy took the fall. The brother was never located, and Warwick Cash ended up with that ring.' He inclined his head. 'Rumour has it the Topaz Stallion only changes hands one way. If that's true, you have your motive.' He tapped the file. 'Cash killed Contanti's brother and took the ring while Jimmy was incarcerated.'

Sam scanned the sheet. The information mirrored what Newman had told him, but one detail jumped out. He looked up at the other man. 'Am I reading this right?'

A slight smile played on Newman's lips.

'Contanti did fifteen years for the Topaz Stallion?'

Newman nodded. 'Apparently it's a national treasure.'

Sam dropped the file on the table. 'The only person that ring has been seen on since is Warwick Cash.'

The older man grinned. 'No shit, Sherlock.' He turned and pointed at the map. 'Cash has recently been sighted in Europe. Interpol was certain he wasn't dead, but they didn't feel it was worthwhile to pursue him. The underworld, on the other hand, thought he was gone. Jimmy and Trafford may not be working together, but they are certainly both after him. I'd put good money on it.' He leant against the desk and folded his arms. 'And you know what that means, Walker?'

Sam felt his earlier anxiety return.

The older man smiled. 'You've got a ticket to ride. We're sending you to Europe.'

Sam shook his head. 'What about Mallory Cash?' He heard the rise in his voice and brought himself under control before continuing. 'Who is going to look for her?'

'We have that in hand, Walker.' Newman pushed away from the desk, his expression uncompromising. 'You're too close to the subject on this one, mate. There's no way we'll let you go looking for her. You want to help Mallory Cash? Stop it at the source. Get on that plane. Go to Europe, apprehend Jimmy Contanti, and as a bonus, let's try to get Trafford in your sights, and take him out of the game, too.'

~

Mallory's excitement started to rise when they reached the outskirts of Sydney. She tried to contain her frustration at the stop-start of peak-hour traffic congestion swelling outwards onto the freeway. She wanted to ask David where they were, but she could see he needed to concentrate on getting the truck through the traffic without mishap.

As they came to a halt at yet another set of lights, he turned to face her. 'I'm not going into the city for love or money at this time of day. I'll take you out the other side near Baulkham Hills. You'll be able to get a train or bus in from there.'

She nodded. 'No problem. I'll figure it out.'

He smiled and started to whistle as he drove. Mallory stared out the window at the cars below and wondered how it felt to live a normal suburban life with a husband, kids, maybe a puppy and a nine-to-five job. She had an image of Sam holding her in his arms, his hands cupping her face, his smile soft before he bent to kiss her, and felt a pang in her stomach. A sudden feeling of loss assailed her, but she had made her decision years ago. Mallory knew she'd never have that kind of life, even though a picket fence, kids, a dog and lazy weekends at the beach seemed very appealing at times.

Right now, however, she had to get herself out of Australia. She would get a new look, a new life and passport, and be on a plane to Europe within forty-eight hours, possibly less if she could access the funds quickly to make it happen. She had contacts in Sydney she could trust, but there was no way of knowing what kind of reception she would receive. It had been a long time, and she knew some would turn their backs on her because she shopped Derek. And what then?

Mallory pulled back from the unknown factors involved in leaving the country, and tracking down her father. She found confidence in knowing that she'd be able to extract more information in Sydney. Mallory had no doubt there were already plenty of rumours circulating about the Topaz Stallion. It was only a matter of working out which one was correct.

3

MALLORY walked out of Kings Cross Station with the confidence of a seasoned Sydney commuter. She waited at the lights, one foot tapping impatiently as she smoothed her pencil skirt and flicked lint off the tailored jacket, looking like any bored office worker on a mid-morning break. The signals changed and she pressed her new glasses onto the bridge of her nose with her index finger before crossing the road. She checked the street sign and turned left toward the internet café in Potts Point. She knew there was always a risk when meeting a contact, but her tension eased as she watched countless pedestrians flowing along the footpath in both directions. Some stared at watches, making silent calculations as they walked, others yelled into phones and looked into the distance without a sidewards glance. It was safe, anonymous; she could disappear into this city easily. When she found the café, she scoped the street and side alley, but there was nothing to suggest a trap. She stepped inside and waited until the crowd around the counter dissipated before approaching the young barista.

The girl grinned at her. 'Whatcha having?'

Mallory ordered a long black and asked, 'Hey, is there

any chance you have a laptop here? I just need to message a friend, and I left mine at the office.' She rolled her eyes and smiled to soften the request.

The barista looked at her blankly, her dark eyes unreadable through thick lashes. Mallory flashed another warm smile and waited. The girl glanced toward the kitchen. 'Just the one message?'

Mallory nodded.

The girl shrugged. 'Yeah, that should be okay, I guess.'

She lifted a laptop onto the bench, typed in the password and pushed it across the counter. Mallory logged onto the *World of Warcraft* website, messaged Ricky and logged off. She flicked open the search history, wiped it and handed the laptop to the girl. 'Thanks so much for that.'

The girl smiled, her face lighting up. 'No problem. Take a seat. I'll bring your coffee in.'

Mallory wandered into the small dining room and sat to one side of the picture window where she could watch pedestrians approaching the café. She knew Ricky would get there as soon as he could, but she wasn't sure of his exact location in Sydney. An older man in reflective aviators, a royal blue beret and a pink jacket that set off his dark skin caught her eye. He was stooped and lean with a neat goatee, his bald head smooth under the jaunty tip of the beret. He moved slowly toward the café and stepped carefully through the open door. He looked vaguely familiar, and as soon as he spoke, she knew it was Ricky. He was a chameleon, but his voice was unmistakeable.

The girl took his order, and he scanned the empty dining room, winking when he caught her eye.

He walked to her table and leaned into her shoulder.

'Lucky you sent a description, *Bella*,' he chuckled.

'Lucky I know your voice anywhere or I would wonder at your audacity, old man,' she laughed.

He let out a bellow of laughter, the rich, strong tones at odds with his frail demeanour.

He placed his coffee and the polished cane he carried on the table, and took her face between his hands. 'How have you been, my beautiful girl?' he asked. He stared into her eyes, his expression unreadable.

She smiled at his flamboyant manner, another thing that did not change with Ricky. 'I've been better, uncle,' she said, dropping her voice slightly.

He slid into the chair opposite and took her hand in his. 'It has been a long time, *ma cherie*.'

She grinned. 'How many languages are you going for, today?'

'As many as it takes to tell you how truly lovely you are.'

She shook her head. 'Always the charmer. Obviously, I've been out of circulation for too long.'

He shifted in his seat. 'Yes, I know. Never thought a Cash would be helping the Heat, though.'

The sudden hard edge to his comment made her realise he had not decided whether he would help her yet. She held his gaze and dropped her voice lower again. 'I get where you're coming from, but it was Derek. He'd already triple-crossed me. I had no choice.'

He bared his teeth in a mirthless grin. 'There's always a choice, even with the stunning Mr James.' He fanned a hand in front of his face and rolled his eyes dramatically. 'I've no doubt that gorgeous specimen is a popular boy in the slammer.'

She snorted and almost choked on her coffee. 'You haven't changed, although you do seem to have gained twenty years from somewhere.'

He sat back, slid the beret off and ran his hand over his glossy, bald head, giving her time to enjoy his disguise. 'This one is a masterpiece, yes?'

She took in his ensemble, nodding her approval at the pink jacket, bright yellow silk shirt and plaid trousers that were set off by shoes the same shade as his beret.

He smiled and took her hand again. 'You are lucky I am here. I went home to Mozambique last week.'

Mallory relaxed. He intended to help her. 'Is everything okay with the family?'

'You know it, sweets, or I wouldn't be here to help you.' He tapped her gently on the hand. 'Though there are plenty who would not help you now, *meu amado*, so take care who you trust.'

She upended her coffee and decided to dive right in. 'But you will help me?'

'That depends on what you need.'

'Information, new ID, and a backstory. The usual.' She paused. 'The problem is, I need it fast. Like, forty-eight hours fast.'

He watched her, his gaze appraising. 'That costs money.'

'I'm good for it.'

'What information?'

'Jimmy Contanti.' She hesitated and looked out the window for a moment, her gaze unfocused. 'And my father, of course.'

An expression of pure anger flashed across his face,

gone as quickly as it occurred. 'There's a lot of stuff bubbling about both of them at the moment.'

Mallory felt a slight fizz of fear. There was something he knew that he wasn't sharing. 'My dad. Is it true that there have been sightings?'

Ricky nodded and glanced around the café. 'Let's not get into this here.'

He squeezed her hand, and she felt the edges of folded paper in her palm. 'Let's meet tomorrow, sweets,' he said with a smile. 'We'll go over old times then.' He drained his coffee and winked at her, his voice soft as velvet. 'Bring the necessaries tomorrow, yes?'

She nodded and watched as he left the café, his ensemble flashing like a bird of paradise through the sea of drab midweek business suits as he shuffled through the crowd and disappeared round the corner.

~

Mallory unlocked the door and stared around the hotel room. It was empty, sterile and anonymous. A heavy depression settled on her as she locked the door behind her. She thought about the gorge and the long afternoon shadows that fell across the artesian spring, the rock wallabies that bounced up the walls and the colourful birds that circled and cried above. She thought about Sam cooking in the warmth of the kitchen, smiling and laughing while his nephew chased lizards on the front porch. That life was so far away now. No going back.

Mallory knew how to hide in hotel rooms, arrange clandestine meetings with old contacts with no guarantees to look forward to, because this had always been her life. One thing that was different was the new level of danger.

She was a target now, and not only for Trafford and Jimmy. She should've known word would be out that she'd shopped Derek to the law. She would have to keep moving, and change her appearance regularly. It was no way to live, but at least it was familiar, and she understood the rules.

She sat down on the edge of the bed and reached her hand under the mattress. She pulled out the pouch she had placed there earlier and slid her pocketknife along one edge. A bank card and licence dropped onto the bed. Mallory inspected the photo. She had never used the alias before and would need to do some work, but it wasn't impossible to get the look right. She tapped the bank card against her palm and smiled. There would be no problem getting the money for tomorrow.

Mallory left the hotel, jumped on a bus to the city and hit the shops. Two hours later she weaved through the afternoon crowds, looking like any other after-work shopper in her smart business suit, her arms laden with bags. The light was beginning to fail and the energy in the city centre was changing. Gone was the anonymous businesslike bustle, replaced by a steady stream of commuters on their way to the ferry terminals and bus stations. Groups of tourists snapped pictures and small knots of girls, their heels clacking in unison, walked toward trendy bars near the water. Young men gathered, their suits long gone, to lounge with open shirts in the long windows at the front of crowded pubs and watch the passing crowd.

Mallory stopped for a moment, eyeing her reflection in a window, and almost laughed out loud. There was no way anyone would recognise her now. She turned away and joined the flow of the crowd along the footpath, letting it carry her toward Circular Quay, as the faint notes of a didgeridoo floated through the air. She followed the sound, stopping when she found the busker. He sat cross-legged, playing with his eyes closed. A pigeon landed on his head and he nodded gently, accommodating the bird without losing his tune. The deep notes vibrated through her, taking her thoughts back to the chilled silence of desert nights in the gorge. She pushed the thoughts away. The busker stopped and opened his eyes. He stared at her and smiled. She dropped coins into his cup and stepped back.

He nodded. 'Thanks. We can't escape the fact that we're all human, eh? Not just a commodity.'

She stopped, glancing around while she considered his words, before nodding in reply. There was no point getting into a philosophical conversation with a stranger, especially if it might lead to extra attention. She wandered to the railing behind him and watched the last rays of the sun lighting up the harbour. It was time to go back to the hotel.

When she reached her room, she folded the clothes she'd bought into a backpack and tried to contain the sudden rush of excitement when she thought about the upcoming meeting with Ricky. Every step of the journey was bringing her closer to finding her father. Closer to understanding why he had abandoned them so many years ago, closer to answers about questions she wasn't even sure she knew yet. A shudder went through her – whether from fear or excitement – at the thought of finally meeting him again.

She walked to the window and pulled the curtain aside. The last of the light was gone from the sky. The lights from the city turned the water in the harbour into a moving, rainbow-coloured palette. She wondered if Sam was out there somewhere in a faceless office, watching the same lightshow on the water and thinking about whether she was safe. She wished she could reach out to him, let him know that she was in no danger. The immediate temptation to find him, to let him know she was safe, was so strong that she shuddered. She closed her eyes and reached out into the universe with her mind, felt the slightest flash of connection. Her eyes snapped open. The feeling seemed so real, but it was only her desire to see Sam that made her want to believe in the impossible.

The risks in contacting him were too high, and besides, he would take her back in and make sure she couldn't go to Europe. Another shudder passed through her, stronger than the first. She moved to the window and stared across the skyline, smiling at the lights twinkling from high-rise buildings across the city. Nothing was going to stop her from finding her father. She may not have a plan for today, but she was ready for whatever was coming her way tomorrow.

~

The next morning, Mallory left her hotel and headed for Paddington, walking along the main road into the suburb until she found the building listed on Ricky's note. She left the road and followed an alley beside the building, stopping at the red door. She rapped three times, as instructed, and waited.

A heavyset man with neck tattoos and enough metal in his face to repair the Titanic opened the door. 'Here for the interview?' he grunted.

She nodded.

He looked her up and down. 'Bar or dancer?'

Trust Ricky! She almost laughed out loud. She knew the answer he would expect. 'Dancer, of course,' she said.

The bouncer raised an eyebrow then shrugged and opened the door to let her through. 'To the right, only door. Make sure you knock.'

He slammed the door behind her and disappeared into darkness of the club.

Mallory stayed where she was and did a quick scan of the hallway. The door to Ricky's office, the door she had come through, and the black depths of the club were the only ways in or out of the hallway. Except for herself, the hallway was empty with no possibility of imminent ambush. She remained alert as she walked to Ricky's door and knocked. The silence in the hall felt almost sentient as she waited, but there was no noise from the other side either. After a few minutes she glanced left and right, the hallway was still deserted. She was tempted to open the door, but she had a feeling the bouncer was a man of few words, so the words he said held weight. He had warned her to knock before entering.

She raised her hand, ready to knock again, when the door swung inward. Ricky stood in the doorway, wearing nothing but a pair of jeans. Even though she knew what a master of disguise he was, she was amazed at the difference in his appearance. His dark skin glowed with health against his white jeans, highlighting defined muscles that rippled as he moved. The extra years he had carried yesterday were gone.

He grinned and signalled to her to enter the room. 'Sorry for making you wait, my darling girl. John is being difficult again, because I didn't take him to Mozambique with me.' He rolled his eyes dramatically and sighed. 'That man can be so needy, don't you think?'

Mallory grinned. 'Stop bullshitting. You love him that way.'

He smirked and waved a hand at her. 'Very true – you know me too well.' He clapped his hands. 'Now, down to business! John can have the ID and backstory ready for you tomorrow. He guarantees the story is bona-fide. There will be no questions asked,' he paused and tapped a finger against the side of his nose, 'unless of course you do something stupid, we can't protect you from that.' He slid into a chair behind a heavy desk in front of a window so grimy that no light shone through. 'Do you need a weapon, sweetheart?'

She shook her head. 'I'm not travelling with a weapon. I'll get one in Europe.'

He nodded. 'Of course. Smart move. I'll make sure you have the right contact there.' He glanced at her and moved a paperweight around on the desk, sliding the glass back and forth over the leather. She realised he was nervous.

'Is everything okay?'

'Well,' he stopped sliding the paperweight and stared directly into her eyes, 'yes and no.' He pointed to the plush armchair in front of the desk. 'Take a seat, sweetheart.'

She looked at the chair dubiously.

He winked. 'Unlike the rest of this club, that chair is quite sanitary. It has never seen any action.'

She laughed and took a seat. 'What's wrong, Ricky?'

He sighed and rubbed a hand across his bare chest. 'There are so many rumours about your father at the moment. He's definitely alive, honey.'

Joy and anger warred within her. If he were alive, why had he never bothered to reach out? Why had he abandoned his family?

'Don't overthink it, sweets,' Ricky said, his deep voice gentle. 'People often have motivations that are not apparent to others.'

She sniffed. 'If you say so.'

Ricky leant back in his chair and draped his long legs across the desk, tapping his pen with metronome precision against his leg. 'Anyway, that's not the issue. There's a lot of buzz around Jimmy the Cat. Word on the street is… he paid you a visit?'

She nodded. 'So, what? You already knew that he did. And yeah, we both know word travels fast.'

'True, that. The question is, what else do *you* know?'

The question hung between them in the silence. Mallory shifted in her chair, unsure where the conversation was going.

'Did you ever hear about the feud over the Topaz Stallion?' Ricky stopped tapping the pen and looked up, his gaze intense.

Mallory frowned, but he'd already dropped his gaze and resumed the metronome tap-tap as he talked. 'It involved two lads from Scotland, the famous Cameron brothers. They disappeared after the Stallion was stolen. Jimmy did time for the job, and somehow your old man turned up with the ring. Now that's enough of a mystery in itself, girl.' He raised an eyebrow before continuing. 'Lately, I've started hearing another rumour about another set of brothers. You see, Warwick and I were tight once. We were practically family, but I never heard him mention a brother.' He stopped talking and contemplated the pen for a moment. 'I mean, I was practically an uncle to you, right?'

She nodded and he eyed her, his expression unreadable. 'Is Jimmy your uncle?'

Mallory burst out laughing. 'Not that I'm aware. If he is, he's the worst uncle in the world. He's attempted to kill me, and he wants to kill my father.'

Ricky dropped the pen on the desk, his expression neutral. 'Well now, we are talking about Jimmy.' He raised an eyebrow. 'And he hasn't killed you yet, has he?'

A cold wave of alarm spread through Mallory. Ricky had known her for all of her life. He had never shown suspicion or hostility, but he was displaying both now.

'What am I missing, Ricky?' she asked.

He leant back in his chair, staring at her through steepled fingers. 'It's like this. I have known your father all my life, and I have always helped you because of that connection. I have been loyal and would never shop you, or yours.' He lifted his legs off the desk and stood in one fluid motion. Mallory was suddenly aware of his size and fitness, of the real physical threat he posed.

'I was shopped five years ago because of Jimmy the Cat. I did six months for that bullshit. Now honey, doing the time don't confront me — the record is nothing more than an inconvenience for me.' He turned his back on her and looked out the window. 'If there were a betrayal… well now, that is another matter.'

She frowned. 'Do you think I'm connected?'

He swung around, his face cold. 'Actually, no. I don't think you are connected to this, but usually Jimmy doesn't "attempt" to kill. It's a competitive sport to him and he knows he's top of his game. He doesn't fail. And you've got form, honey. You shopped Derek to the Heat. Maybe I was wrong about your father? Maybe you learnt a thing or two observing your old man—'

Cold alarm turned into icy fingers, gripping Mallory's gut, squeezing her heart, making it hard to think. 'But I don't understand? Why would my father want to hurt you—'

'I will help you get to Europe,' Ricky interrupted.

In two strides, he was standing over her chair. 'Because we have history, and I gave my word.' He towered over her. She wanted to stand, acutely aware of her vulnerability. She stayed seated, hoping he couldn't see the sweat breaking out along her hairline and on her top lip. She resisted the urge to wipe the sweat away, locking her arms by her side and her mounting fear deep inside. She kept all her senses attuned to Ricky. It wouldn't do to show weakness.

He leant over, placing his hands either side of the armchair, his face inches from hers, and whispered, 'It seems Bruges is the place to be. It's turning into quite a party over there.' He stood up and let out a baritone roll of laughter. 'Word is, Interpol are wetting themselves in five different directions because Jimmy and Trafford are heading for Bruges. A little birdie is insisting Eve Saldino is on her way too.' He raised both perfectly manicured eyebrows. 'Now there's an explosive three-way that will get the fur flying.'

His sudden change of tack threw her. 'What do you mean by that?'

'Damn girl, Jimmy and Eve have some history, too. You've never heard?' He threw his head back and started to laugh. He kept going until Mallory started to wonder if he was hysterical.

He stopped suddenly, his face a mixture of mistrust and concern. 'I was shopped for something that I thought only Warwick knew. Now, if Jimmy is his brother, that changes everything for me.' He moved back to his desk and sank into his chair, resting his chin on his hands as he looked at her, his expression grave. 'Believe me, my dear, if they are brothers, it will change everything for you. You will be in more danger than you ever thought possible. Everyone will be coming at you to even some scores.'

She frowned. 'But—'

Ricky held up one hand. 'No, let's not worry about that possibility. Let's focus on getting you safely to Europe. The rest will come out in the wash.'

Mallory left the club with Ricky's words ringing in her ears. She thought about Jimmy, his actions, the way he looked, how easily he killed. There was no way that he could be her father's brother. There was absolutely no way she could be related to someone as cold and heartless as Jimmy the Cat. She racked her brain for any memory of Jimmy from her childhood, but she knew she would not find one. It was a stupid theory with no factual basis. She shook her head and turned her thoughts to the future. Ricky had promised to have the ID and cash at the club by lunchtime tomorrow. She knew it was risky to return after their conversation, but she had no other choice if she wanted to get out of Sydney. She would have to trust him at his word, and hope that he didn't have a change of heart overnight.

She decided to be prepared to flee. She would book the flight to Bruges as soon as she had the new passport. It wasn't safe to hang around in Sydney with so many rumours swirling, and there was the added complication of her own actions with Derek. She wondered if Sam had already briefed Interpol on Jimmy's visit. Not that it would do them any good. Everyone knew the law was always five steps behind. She flicked on the cheap phone she'd purchased earlier in the day and found the nearest library. She may not be able to make plans until tomorrow, but she would find out everything she could about the city she was about to visit.

~

Sam left the office and fought his way against the swelling crowd of pedestrians streaming toward Circular Quay. He checked his watch and decided to wait until the afternoon rush settled. He stepped into the next bar he encountered, ordered a drink and took a seat at the window facing the Quay. He stared blindly into the moving crowd on the footpath, his thoughts circling back to Mallory. He had the strongest feeling she was safe, but he couldn't explain why or how he could think such a thing. Yet, he couldn't shake the feeling they were connected, and he believed he would know if something final had happened to her. Sudden doubt assailed him. An image of her alone and dying in the desert flashed into his mind. All her captors had to do was leave her in an isolated place away from a road, and she would die without any wounds inflicted. He shook his head, focusing his gaze on the flowing crowd outside to distract his mind from spiralling into panicked speculation.

Some of the passing commuters were worn and tired, their frustration at the endless pushing and rushing apparent on their faces. Some were excited, like puppies just released from cages, and others were still in work mode, gesticulating into the air as they talked business on their phones. Most were dressed in smart, conservative office attire. He watched a group of middle-aged men pass with mild interest. They went against the trend, dressed in white t-shirts, jeans and casual blazers, accessorised with Converse sneakers, yin and yang jewellery, expensive watches and aviator sunglasses. There was no doubt these were advertising types, creatives who refused to conform and yet still conformed to their own stereotype.

His thoughts returned to Mallory again. He felt a sudden closeness to her and wondered at the rationality of his thinking. There was no reason to believe she was in Sydney, or even safe, for that matter. There had been no word from the office and if anything changed, he knew he would be informed immediately. He checked his watch. This time tomorrow afternoon, he would be on a flight to Bruges, but he didn't hold much hope of her being found before he left. He looked into the dregs of his beer and silently crossed his fingers around the base of his glass. All he could do was hope she would find a way to protect herself, because it was impossible to fight directives from above. All the same, it didn't seem right to leave Australia while she was still missing.

He took the last draught of his beer and considered his limited options. The brief he'd been given earlier was extensive, but it was riddled with rumours and speculation. There had been a sighting of Jimmy Contanti in Bruges within the last two days, so he, at least, was not an immediate threat to Mallory. The rumours were swirling that Warwick Cash may be in Bruges as well. And there was talk that Trafford was headed there too. All because of an old vendetta that appeared to be linked to the Topaz Stallion. He frowned. It was a beautiful ring, but there had to be more to the story than the mere ownership of one ring.

He looked up, his gaze barely focused on the crowd outside as he considered the implications of the presence of three notorious jewel thieves in Bruges. A blonde woman on the other side of the street caught his eye. She was dressed in a navy suit, cream blouse and flat, sensible shoes. Her walk was relaxed but brisk, her legs swung out with a little kick at the knee, and her head tilted just so. It was only a glimpse, a mere outline in the deepening dusk, but he felt certain he had just seen Mallory. His eyes widened as she disappeared into a scrum of tourists marching toward the Opera House. He jumped off the bar stool and ran out into the milling crowd on the footpath. A group of women stopped in front of him, laughing and high-fiving as they parted for the day. He squeezed past them and stared in the direction of the woman, but she was dressed like all the other people leaving their offices and was nowhere to be seen.

He pulled out his phone and dialled the super. 'Sir, has there been any word?'

'No. Believe me, we are taking this seriously, Walker.' The super paused. 'If she's out there, we'll find her.'

Sam hung up and thought about the woman he'd just seen. It had to be wishful thinking on his part. There was no way she could have made it to Sydney without even a whisper of her movements coming back through to Intelligence. He decided that he wanted Mallory to be alive and safe so badly that he was projecting her mannerisms onto strangers, but a niggling doubt remained. He peered into the thickening crowd one more time and then turned away. There was no point chasing shadows. He had to put her out of his mind and get some sleep. He would need his wits about him when he landed in Bruges.

~

Mallory stepped into the library and stopped for a moment to enjoy the muted whisper of paper and voices, the hum of photocopiers and smell of old books and newspapers. The library had been her favourite place when she was a teenager. Through all the years her mother had struggled to keep food on the table, the library, so warm and inviting, had been her escape. There were limitless stories to choose from, the perfect release from nagging hunger pains and the seeping cold that seemed to invade every corner of their home. She would stay for hours, reading stories of lost children reunited with their parents and imagining the day when her family would be reunited. There was always a happy ending, and the tales of love and plenty fuelled her desire to see her father return. Her fantasies had so consumed her that she was sure she had false images of him buried in her memories. She could see him now, knocking on the door and opening his arms to scoop her up into a huge bear hug; or arriving in a large, luxurious car, laden with gifts and compliments; or walking her toward a field with a horse, just for her. They played past her inner eye like a movie, so apparently real, and yet she knew they were not. All her fantasies of the perfect family were fostered by the books she had read at the library. She smiled at her naïve, childish hopes, but a small dart of excitement passed through her, too. If the rumours were true, a reunion with her father might be possible after all. But first, she had to be prepared.

Mallory walked toward the travel section and ran her finger along the books as she browsed. The best place to start would be a Lonely Planet guide for Bruges. Once she had a handle on the basics, she would study maps, local hangouts, places of interest, cuisine, the way people dressed, the way they walked and talked. Then she would dive deeper and look at politics, policing and government policies. She would study everything that was needed to look like a person who had a reason to visit.

4

SAM clipped the seat belt around his waist and stared out the window of the plane. A woman dumped her bag on the aisle seat on his row and stowed a pair of crutches in the compartment. He gave her a quick smile when she sat down beside him and turned back to the sullen afternoon outside, with its threatening sky. He watched the balloons that measured wind direction and velocity billow and fill as heavy gusts of wind hit them, and wondered if the plane would be allowed to fly. The howl of the engines lifted another notch as he searched for something natural, some familiar sign of the landscape he loved so much. There was only glass, tarmac and concrete as far as the eye could see. He knew it was merely an overcast autumn day, but the grey farewell from Sydney did not bode well for the journey ahead. He pushed the superstitious thoughts away. It wasn't like him to dwell on negatives or look for signs in random events. It wasn't like him to miss the inland country of his childhood so badly when he had a job to do. A wave of tiredness washed over him, and his eyes felt heavy. He was homesick and he'd slept badly.

The woman beside him cleared her throat. He turned

to her and she pointed at a cast on her wrist. 'I'm sorry to be a bother. Do you mind if I use your arm rest?'

He shook his head. 'Looks like you've been in the wars.'

'Yes,' she said. 'An electric scooter accident. Yesterday.' She rolled her eyes. 'Talk about bad timing.' She elevated one leg as far as she could. 'At least I didn't break my leg, but my ankle isn't happy.'

He winced in sympathy at her bandaged ankle and picked up the safety magazine to signal the conversation was over. He skimmed the steps needed to ensure a person exited the plane safely, and wondered how many people actually bothered to listen when the instructions were explained. After all, there was every chance a person was dead if the plane plummeted into the seas. He shook his head to derail the negative turn his thoughts were taking again. The depressed weather and the continued absence of Mallory was taking more of a toll than he realised.

The doors thumped shut and the seat belt warning chimed before the plane started to taxi. Sam leant back into his seat with a sigh. He folded his long legs into the cramped space between the seats to avoid ramming his knees into the seat in front. The jet accelerated, the roar and shake of the engines matching the turmoil he felt within. A baby started crying two rows ahead and the hissing whispers of a couple fighting broke out behind him. The flight would be hell for sure. The best thing to do was sleep. That way, he would be ready for whatever came his way when he landed in Bruges. The plane levelled and the woman beside him pushed the armrest down. He felt the cast on her wrist press into his side, and moved his body away. He closed his eyes, and an image of Mallory sunbaking beside the spring in the gorge sprang onto the back of his eyelids. It was so vivid, his breath caught in his throat. She turned sideways, smiled at him and said, 'Hey, you. I knew you'd come find me.'

His eyes snapped open and he looked around the cabin. His body shook, and his breathing came in short breaths. He'd been dreaming, but she'd felt so close, it was almost as if she were sitting beside him. But of course, she wasn't there. What if she were already dead, and would only ever come to him in his dreams now? Perhaps that was why she seemed so real, and so close. Tears pricked at the back of his eyes and he lifted his fists, pressing them into his sockets. There was no point dwelling on possibilities. His current state of mind was dangerous. He had to break it.

'Stop it, Walker,' he whispered.

As the engines changed and the jet started to cruise, Sam felt his resolve give way. Mallory had been out in the cold for too long. The women who had taken her were professional killers. He had to accept that he would never see her again. Silent tears seeped over his fists and ran down his face.

~

The jet banked and levelled, and the seat belt lights blinked out. Mallory pressed a button and extended the leg rest. She looked at the space around her and thanked God for hidden bank accounts – first or business was the only way to travel in the air. Her thoughts turned to Sam. He was no doubt desperately scouring inland Australia for her right now. She felt a stab of guilt, but it was short-lived. If she had contacted him, he would have insisted that she turn herself in, and he may have convinced her. She would have been stuck in a safe house that was anything but safe, while her father faced Jimmy the Cat alone. She knew Sam would worry about her safety, but he had already proven he would choose the law over her. No, she was better off going it alone and finding her father. She imagined Sam walking around the gorge, covering the ground in long, loping strides, his keen eyes missing nothing. He would quickly realise what she had done the night before she left. Others would not notice her trail, but she knew he would piece it together. Not that it would do him any good now. He wouldn't be able to follow her trail past the roadhouse, and she could never go back to the gorge, would never see him or his family again. It made her want to pick up the glass of champagne the steward had placed on her tray and smash it against the window. She wanted to cry and scream at the unfairness of it all, but that chapter of her life was over, so what was the point?

Her thoughts turned toward her next destination. She picked up her phone and checked her appearance. The disguise was one of the best she'd ever done, and the passport John organised was flawless. She was Anita Maybury, a travel blogger and fashion influencer, the kind of person who travelled regularly and took photos at every opportunity. She snapped a selfie and stared at the image. Anita looked nothing like her real self, but it wouldn't hurt to use some extra filters. She played around with the photo before uploading it to her new Instagram account. No one expected Mallory Cash to be in Bruges, and no one would expect her to choose a profession that included posting photos online and sharing her current location. It was a bold move, but she trusted the disguise would hold up to scrutiny. She felt confident that anyone who mattered would not recognise her online. Besides, the disguise would only be needed for a few days in Bruges. She stared at the likes ticking over on her Instagram feed and grinned. As soon as she secured a new identity in Bruges, Anita Maybury would suffer a tragic accident.

~

After the plane reached altitude and the seatbelt lights went out, a steward approached Sam and tapped him on the shoulder.

'Excuse me, Sir,' she whispered. 'We have an upgrade to first class. We have been instructed to offer it to you.'

Sam smiled at the thought of stretching out his already-stiff legs. He imagined lying back and having a proper sleep in first class. He was on the point of accepting when he glanced at the woman next to him. Her eyes were closed but she looked uncomfortable and was probably in pain.

He turned back to the steward and shook his head. 'Can you offer my place to the lady next to me, please? She's injured and in pain.'

The steward's eyes widened in surprise before she nodded.

'Probably best that you wake her,' he said. He turned toward the window, watching out of the corner of his eye as the steward woke the woman and informed her that she was being moved to first class. He saw the relief on the woman's face and knew he made the right decision. At any rate, he wouldn't have to put up with the cast digging into his side for the rest of the flight. He closed his eyes and pushed the seat back as far as it would go, letting his arms drop on to both vacant rests. He decided to try and get some more sleep. It was going to be a long flight.

~

At the front of the plane, the steward pulled the curtain back and led a woman on crutches into the first-class cabin. They stopped at the seat across the aisle from Mallory.

The woman glanced over, caught Mallory's eye and smiled. 'Hi. I've never travelled first before. I was just told the kind man sitting beside me in cattle gave me his upgrade.' A slight blush rose up her neck and cheeks as she spoke. 'And he was so handsome. Skin like manuka honey and the greenest eyes I've ever seen.' She grinned wider as she flapped her hands back and forth, as if fanning an overheated face.

An image of Sam's green eyes, full of laughter and cheek, flashed through Mallory's mind. She smiled in return. 'Good to know there are some gentlemen left.'

The woman stared at her, suddenly intent. 'Has anyone told you that you look a lot like Anita Maybury?'

A jolt of shock passed through Mallory. She hadn't expected to be identified quite so quickly. Perhaps a high-profile backstory was not the best idea after all. She was considering lying when she realised the woman was looking at the last Instagram post she'd uploaded.

'Oh my God, you're Anita Maybury!' The woman stepped closer. 'I'm so sorry, you must get sick of people asking you that,' she gushed.

Mallory shook her head. 'It's totally fine. Goes with the territory.'

The woman frowned, her gaze penetrating. 'You look different, though, like something has changed.' She kept staring with such intensity that Mallory felt alarmed.

She leant back in her seat and shrugged. 'Well filters,

you know. We all use them. I'm always surprised to be recognised at all.'

The woman stepped back. 'I'm being rude. Of course, you would use filters and photoshop. All the best ones do.'

Mallory heard a note of disbelief in the woman's voice. She watched her arrange her belongings and slide into her seat, and cursed the kind gentleman who had sent her to first class. It was going to be a long journey with stopovers – she didn't need a new friend. She laid her seat back and closed her eyes, blocking out all thoughts of the mission she faced in Europe, and drifted into a semi-dream state.

~

The next day, Mallory kept her elation in check as the plane started to descend through thick grey clouds. She lifted her seat into an upright position, and leant against the window to get a better view of the streets of Bruges below. Perhaps her father was somewhere down there right now, looking up between the buildings, watching the plane descend, unaware that his daughter was on board. If not, she felt certain the contact Ricky had arranged in Sydney would lead her to him. Finding him seemed as inevitable as breathing now. Excitement welled within her and she let out a sigh in an effort to contain her emotions.

'It is beautiful, isn't it?'

Mallory almost jumped at the sound of a voice so close to her. She glanced behind her seat and saw the woman with the crutches standing in the space between her seat and the empty one behind her, peering out the window beside her own. She looked down at the densely packed buildings with their red roofs, red brick chimneys and whitewash. It was beautiful in its own way, but it didn't compare to the

Rockies on a bright winter day. She felt a pang at the thought of Canada. It had been so long since she had stepped on home soil. The pang deepened into depression at the thought of exile. It was possible she may never be able to return and witness the clear winter sun bouncing off the pristine snow that covered the jagged mountains of her childhood home. She focused on the city, closer now — steepled churches, bunched terraces and canals came into focus among the rows of roofs. It wouldn't be long before she would be walking those streets, crossing those canals, making her way toward her father.

'What brings you to Bruges?'

Mallory glanced at the woman, hiding her annoyance behind a smile. 'Family.'

The other woman shifted on her crutches. Mallory noticed muscles rippling under her t-shirt. Her movements were lithe, despite her injuries. Something about her features and the way she pulled one side of her mouth down as she tucked a stray hair behind her ear, the familiarity of it niggled. 'And you? Business or pleasure?' Mallory asked.

The woman smiled. 'As you can see, not pleasure.' She looked out the window again, her face expressionless. 'Also family.'

'Must be the year for it,' Mallory said.

The warning lights in the cabin started to flash and the woman smiled and flicked her a tiny wave before returning to her seat.

Mallory thought about the woman's gestures. There was something about her, but she couldn't place it. She pushed her anxiety down as she buckled her seatbelt and decided that the situation was making her jumpy.

~

At the back of the plane, Sam also turned away from the view of Bruges and adjusted his belt. He ticked over the information given to him in Sydney. An operative from the Belgian Federal Police would be waiting at the airport to escort him to Interpol headquarters. Once there, the hunt for Jimmy Contanti would start in earnest. The only problem he could foresee was the lack of evidence to back up his theory. He couldn't be sure what the connection was, but Jimmy Contanti and Warwick Cash had history. He had no doubts that Jimmy the Cat would lead him to Warwick Cash and the Topaz Stallion. He hoped that whatever he discovered would lead him back to Mallory. He couldn't accept never seeing her again, he just couldn't. He had to keep believing that he would find her. He had to believe she was alive and safe. He couldn't function otherwise. Sam leant back and closed his eyes, his mind already on the job ahead as the plane dropped toward the runway.

~

The jet landed on the tarmac with a thud, cracking Mallory's teeth together with the impact. She rolled her eyes and cursed the pilot. The engines howled under the pressure of slowing the aircraft's trajectory, and her knuckles tightened on the armrest. This was her least favourite part of flying. The plane finally slowed and turned, taxiing toward the terminal. She relaxed in her seat. There was no rush. She would wander through duty free, wait on her baggage – do everything a tourist with plenty of time and nowhere to be would do. After the safety lights stopped flashing, she stood, collected her hand luggage, and steadied her growing excitement at the thought of finding her father.

When she started toward the exit, the woman on crutches followed her. 'I'm always so happy to get out of a plane after a long flight,' she laughed.

Mallory shrugged. 'Yeah. I don't have anywhere to be, though.' The woman's mannerisms and her over-friendliness bothered her. She increased her pace in the tunnel leading from the plane to the terminal and let herself be pushed along by the crowds threading through duty free. She wandered around in a perfume shop and stopped behind a display to watch the passenger from first class hobble past on her crutches. When people bumped and jostled the woman, her expression hardened, and her body language looked dangerous, causing more than one commuter to shrink away from her. Mallory had a lightning flash of recognition, gone too quickly. She couldn't place it. She knew that there were plenty of people in the world who looked alike, but that momentary flash alarmed her. The strange woman seemed familiar for all the wrong reasons. Mallory knew it didn't pay to ignore her gut. She watched until the woman was out of sight and exited the shop in the opposite direction.

~

Sam waited beside the baggage carousel, watching bags appear under the plastic strips, roll around the carousel and disappear back into the bowels of the building. He knew the bags would take some time to appear and figured he should reach out to his contact, but he wanted time to get his bearings. He felt someone stop beside him, too close for comfort, and stepped away.

'Oh, sorry. I didn't mean to crowd you.' The woman with the crutches beamed at him. 'I'm glad I found you. I wanted to say thank you.'

He smiled easily. 'Don't mention it.'

She moved closer, almost touching him. 'The steward told me you gave the upgrade to me. I'd be happy to buy you a drink, a meal even, if you're in town for a while. To repay the favour.'

Something in her expression, the way she half-smiled, reminded him of Mallory. The thought stalled him for a minute, his mind returning to the possibility of Mallory in danger. He dragged himself back to the present. The woman leaned closer and placed a hand on his forearm. She took his silence as assent and squeezed his arm, making no attempt to disguise the hungry intention behind her offer. He decided he was mistaken. She looked nothing like Mallory.

He shifted his arm away from her touch. 'That's really kind, but I won't be here long enough to take you up on the offer, thanks.'

She raised an eyebrow. 'Oh wow! I do love that gorgeous Aussie accent.'

'Thanks.'

She nodded. 'Well thank you, once again. You really are a gentleman.'

He nodded in return, relieved when she moved along the carousel to collect her bag.

After she moved away, he collected his bag and walked toward the main exit, scanning the crowd for his contact. He saw the operative at the same time she saw him. They nodded and walked without speaking toward a car waiting outside the door.

She slid into the back seat beside him, tapping the

driver's headrest before turning and holding out her hand. 'Martine Berg.'

Sam shook her hand and clipped his belt on as the driver accelerated into the heavy traffic. 'Sam Walker.'

Martine smiled. 'We have an office ready for you, but you may not be here long. Jimmy Contanti appears to be on the move.'

Sam's hunter instinct kicked in. 'Any idea where he's headed?'

Martine glanced at her watch. 'It appears he is intending to catch a ferry to Scotland.'

Sam frowned. 'Scotland? What's of interest there?'

She looked out the window as they slowed and halted at a set of lights. 'We cannot be sure. One of Trafford Sykes' men arrived in Bruges yesterday.' She turned back to Sam. 'He appears to be tracking Contanti. We're not entirely sure why at this stage.'

'And the connection to Warwick Cash?'

Martine stared at him, her eyes wide. 'Warwick Cash? There have been rumours about the Topaz Stallion, and yes, they centre around Cash, but we have no reason to believe he is connected to Contanti's present movements.' She flicked her wrist and checked her watch. 'We will require a full debrief on Contanti's movements in Australia.'

Sam nodded, but he wasn't inclined to agree with her about Warwick. Jimmy the Cat had travelled to Australia with the specific intention of finding Mallory and telling her about her father. If he were intending to travel to Scotland, Sam had no doubt that the trip would be connected to Warwick Cash.

~

The baggage carousel was deserted by the time Mallory arrived. She saw her bag disappear under the plastic and grabbed it when it reappeared again. She headed toward the bus terminal outside the airport, found the service for the Ezelstraat Quarter, climbed onto the bus and pulled a crumpled piece of paper out of her pocket. She stared at the number for a moment, before rolling the paper into a ball and squashing it out of sight between the seat cushions. Ricky had assured her the contact in Bruges would help her, but after their last meeting she wasn't inclined to fully trust any connection Ricky offered. She thought about her options and decided it was time to call in some favours. She looked out the window at the crowd streaming along the footpath outside the terminal. The woman on crutches hobbled past, slowing as she came to the front of the bus. Mallory held her breath, letting out a sigh of relief when the woman turned and kept walking toward another bus station. She watched until she was out of sight, aware once again that her mannerisms seemed unsettlingly familiar. Then the bus pulled away from the terminal and Mallory forgot the strange woman, already deep in planning her next move as the bus moved through the streets and over the canals of Bruges.

~

Mallory leant on the stone wall and watched swans drifting on the water below the bridge. Stone buildings flanked the canal in stately silence, the lack of traffic giving the area an aura of old-world tranquillity. She smiled at the ordered beauty of the place, so different from the beauty of the outback gorge she'd called home for so many months, and worlds away from the frozen magnificence of the Canadian

Rockies. She checked her watch and glanced at a couple strolling, ice creams in hand, on the path on one side of the bridge. They stopped and kissed briefly, their laughter floating across the water as they started walking again. A pang went through her at the sight of them. She would never enjoy such simple pleasures, but she still had time to make like a tourist. She walked the length of the bridge, trailing a hand along the rough stone wall. Her back was to the canal when she stopped and turned, taking a selfie, like any visitor to the city on a day trip. She scanned the street. The young lovers were gone. A dog sniffed an overturned rubbish bin near the mouth of the alley, and a taxi cruised past, the driver slowing to see if she intended to signal. Otherwise, there was no sign of life, despite the medieval beauty of the district.

She crossed the cobbled street and slowed to look at a series of lithographs in the window of an art gallery. They were intricate, the delicate lines revealing layer after layer of meaning. She stepped away from the window, resisting the dangerous urge to sink further into the art. After glancing either side of the road and finding it still empty, she slipped into the alley, keeping her body relaxed and her breathing even. The area may look deserted, but she had no doubt her contact, Linus, would have taken precautions – there was a good chance she was being watched as she made her way to the rendezvous point. She walked along the alley and exited through an arch into a large courtyard. The hairs on the back of her neck lifted. The windowless façade of the buildings facing the courtyard showed no sign of watchers, but there was a definite sensation of eyes on her. She stepped to one side and studied the grey walls surrounding the courtyard until she saw the concealed camera she expected to find. She moved into the shadows along one wall, watching the camera track her movements as she headed toward the door at the other end. No doubt she was expected, but it still gave her a slight jump when the door swung open while she was halfway along the wall. There was no cover to be found, but she refused to show fear.

A tall, slim man with intricate symbols tattooed on his face, similar to the lithographs in the gallery window, appeared. His skin was almost translucent against the black of the tattoos, his hair and eyebrows white. He appeared albino until he removed his sunglasses and revealed deep brown eyes and black lashes. He watched her walk toward him, his head cocked to one side and hands hooked into his jeans' pockets. Mallory's body coiled in readiness to spring into action if he showed any aggression, but he appeared relaxed.

She stopped out of reach and held out both hands, palms up. 'I'm here to see Linus.'

He gave her a lopsided grin. 'Well, of course you are, my dear. Follow me.' He turned away and walked into the darkness beyond the door.

Mallory hesitated. Entering a building with an unknown contact was extremely risky. It could be a setup; it could be mistaken information. There were so many variables to consider, and more than one of them could mean this would be the last building she ever entered. But it was also the only way she could get what she needed in Bruges. She stepped into the doorway and waited for her eyes to adjust. The man stood quite still, his pale skin and white hair glowing in the pooling darkness of the interior. There didn't appear to be anyone else in the room.

He curled an index finger. 'Come, my lady.'

The door behind her swung shut. She whirled to face a possible threat, but there was nobody there.

Linus let out a low, dry laugh at her reaction. 'Automatic door, Miss.' He held up a hand and pointed his index finger at her and pulled an imaginary trigger. 'If I wanted to kill you, I would have done so in the courtyard.'

His soft, cultured voice was so at odds with the words coming out of his mouth that Mallory almost grinned, but this was no comedy.

She heard a click and light flooded, revealing a large room with high ceilings. He flicked another button and a panel slid across the ceiling, revealing a huge domed skylight at the apex of the roof comprised of ornate stained glass. She gasped at the sight.

'It's bloody amazing, isn't it? I think this place may have been a chapel once.' He gave a short, barking laugh. 'One imagines they would be rolling in their graves.'

He slipped on a pair of square reading glasses and walked to a bank of computers against one wall, tapping buttons and making low whistles as though he were alone. He looked around, his expression guarded. 'There's been a glitch in the matrix, my lady. You will have to wait a week.'

'Why?'

'Reasons beyond my control.' He clicked a button and the glowing screens powered down. He leant against the computer and stared at her. She held her nerve against the sudden silence and his scrutiny.

'There's word on the street about the Topaz Stallion and two feuding brothers. Where do you fit in?'

She shook her head. 'I don't. I know nothing about a feud.'

He folded his arms across his chest. 'If you do not fit in, why would you be chasing a loose cannon like Jimmy, then?'

Mallory knew people were talking, but his words still jolted her. She kept her face impassive.

He pushed away from the bench, stepping closer to her. 'Unless of course the old stories are true?'

She shook her head. 'I don't know anything about the old stories either.'

He arched an eyebrow, his expression suddenly arctic. 'Really? The story goes, the Topaz Stallion was stolen by the Cameron brothers, a pair of up-and-coming hopefuls from Scotland. Did you know Trafford had the Topaz Stallion for almost thirty years? He took it off the dead hand of his first boss.' He stroked his chin. 'Legend goes, he only lost it because he trusted the wrong person to return it to him — one of the Cameron brothers.' He grinned at her expression. 'It really is news to you, isn't it?'

He returned to the computers and started typing. Old newspaper reports flashed up on a screen. 'Take a look at this. After Trafford got double-crossed, the Topaz Stallion was held in the possession of the French Government for two weeks.' He let out short barks of laughter. 'Apparently, the French did not see it coming. Everyone thought the Cameron brothers had pulled off the perfect heist.'

He flicked open another site and pointed at a photo of Jimmy the Cat. 'But here's where it gets strange. The Cameron brothers never owned it, and they certainly never fenced it. They just disappeared, and so did the Topaz

Stallion. Jimmy the Cat had to be involved for sure, because he got shopped for that job. Then the Topaz Stallion suddenly reappeared on Warwick Cash's hand. Now, it's no secret your old man ended up with the ring, but it is the *how* that has always had people stumped.'

He turned and pointed his hand at her, shaping it into a gun again. 'The word is out that you shopped Derek James to the Heat in Australia, and then disappeared off the planet.' He pulled his trigger finger, mouthing a silent 'pow' before continuing. 'So, it begins to look like your family has form in that department, because if your father didn't shop Jimmy for that ring, then how did he get that ring? And if it wasn't Warwick, then who had reason to shop the Cat over the ring? The lost Cameron brothers? It certainly wasn't Trafford – he would sort his business the old-fashioned way.'

He dropped his arm, his expression genuinely perplexed. 'But why? And where do they fit in anyway?' He stared hard at her. 'And now the Topaz Stallion *and* your old man resurface together, and here *you* are.'

'But, I don't know—'

He shook his head. 'Sucks to be you, and sucks to be out of the loop. Things have changed since you contacted me. I can't help.'

A blast of cold air hit her as the door swung open. She had so many questions, and couldn't help turning back to Linus one more time. 'But wha—'

He held up his hands. 'Do not ask any questions!' He contemplated her in silence before spreading his hands wide. 'Look, word is, Jimmy is on his way to Scotland. If you decide to go, there's a man, Petey, in Edinburgh. He isn't connected to anyone that matters. He will help you for the right price.' He pulled a sheet of paper off a notepad near the computer. 'This is the information for the contact.'

He passed it to her, and she rolled it into her fist. He folded his arms across his chest and inclined his head toward the exit. The interview was over.

She hesitated again on the threshold, wanting to ask more questions, but the door was already swinging shut behind her. She moved across the courtyard with a new urgency, her legs shaking as fear hit. Trafford had to be in the mix. There was no doubt Linus refused to help her because her old boss was on his way to Bruges. She was confused too, over the story about the Cameron brothers. She couldn't work out how her father or Jimmy the Cat fit in, and why it should affect her. She didn't have the full story, but she felt certain that the answers she needed would be found in Scotland.

~

Mallory returned to the Ezelstraat Quarter, and realised her stomach was making almost as much noise as her troubled thoughts. She found a small restaurant and scanned the crowd while she waited for her meal. The venue was full of well-dressed young women enjoying slow lunches – the perfect place for her particular disguise. When her meal arrived, she turned her attention to the bowl of mussels, dipping her fries into the broth with enjoyment.

A shadow fell over the table and she looked up, silently cursing when she realised it was the woman on crutches. The woman smiled at her, and a prickle of apprehension passed through her. She had scanned the restaurant when she arrived, and the woman had not been there.

'Hey Anita, you were on the plane with me. In first class?' The woman's voice boomed across the restaurant, and several women at tables nearby turned to stare.

Mallory flinched inwardly but kept her face and body still. She frowned, feigning ignorance. 'I did catch a flight here in the last couple of days, yes. But I'm sorry, I don't remember you.'

The other woman watched her, her eyes narrow, a slight, predatory smile on her face. Mallory felt another stab of recognition. The woman's expression reminded her of someone.

The silence between the pair continued until the woman shifted awkwardly on her crutches. 'My bad. I thought you'd be sure to remember me because of my crutches, and you know, first class... I guess it's a minor celebrity thing, ignoring others, yeah?' She smirked.

Mallory shrugged, signalling the conversation was over. She returned her attention to her lunch, but the woman remained beside the table.

'By the way, did you find your family?' she asked.

Mallory kept eating, taking her time before she made eye contact again. She remembered the conversation clearly. She had told the woman she was in Bruges on family business, she had never mentioned trying to find anyone. Every nerve in her body was on red alert. It could be a slip of the tongue, but there was something about the woman's expression, and her insistent questioning, that bothered her.

She smiled a wide, warm smile. 'Having a close family is the best, isn't it?'

The woman's face closed, and her lips flattened into a bitter line, making her appear much older than her years.

She shrugged. 'I wouldn't know about that.'

Mallory refused to be drawn into further conversation and turned back to her lunch, listening to the uneven clop of the crutches as the woman hopped away. She turned her features over in her mind, trying to find a match, but complete recognition still eluded her. She continued her lunch, taking her time, aware that the other woman was somewhere behind her in the restaurant. Ten minutes passed and she leaned back and signalled for the bill. After she paid, she resisted the urge to turn and locate the unknown woman in the restaurant. The last thing she wanted to do was show any interest. She had no idea who she was, but she was certain she had an agenda.

Mallory stepped onto the street outside the restaurant, shaken by the encounter with the stranger. She didn't believe in coincidences. The woman on crutches had popped up more than once now, and the unsettling familiarity in her mannerisms, the way her mouth was set, told her there was danger involved, and Linus had made it quite clear she was already on borrowed time. The risks appeared to be multiplying.

She had to get out of Bruges as quickly as possible. The longer she stayed in one place, the more likely her disguise would be compromised. She decided to travel to France and catch the ferry to Scotland from Zeebrugge. Once there, she could find Linus' man, Petey, in Edinburgh, buy a new passport, change her look and get a watertight backstory. Her current disguise was obviously too risky – even if she tried to throw people off the trail, every photo she posted could be used to get one step closer to her. Mallory stepped up against the wall of a shop and opened the gallery on her phone. She chose the last photo she'd taken, edited the background to a different Quarter in Bruges, and captioned the shot, "Quality family time for the next few weeks – I may not be online as often, but I'll still be thinking about my lovely tribe of followers." She hit the post button and started walking again, scanning the lunchtime crowd, ready to avoid the woman if she saw her.

A tall, dark-haired man stepped out of a café onto the pavement ahead of her, and stopped for a moment with his back to her. She gasped, stopping dead. It seemed impossible, but her eyes were not deceiving her. He turned and started walking in her direction, and her breath caught at the sight. Memories from the gorge swamped her – the outback heat, the colourful birds rising into cloudless skies, the dust, the cicada racket and smell of eucalypt on the air returned for a moment, blocking out the chill wind and grey skies over Bruges. He was oblivious to her presence as he checked his watch, before stopping for a moment when a passer-by spoke to him. He smiled and her heart skipped.

She turned away before he had a chance to see her, staring blindly at row after row of glossy pastries and fluffy cakes in a bakery window. She stepped closer to the window, her forehead almost touching the cold glass, her shoulders hunched, making herself as small and nondescript as possible. Someone stopped behind her, and even before the smell of his cologne hit, her body recognised his. A hot flush rose, flooding her cheeks. Her heartbeat accelerated. Every nerve ending responded to his presence, but surely it was impossible that he had seen her? He was still behind her, neither moving nor speaking. Perhaps he was unaware of her presence? Maybe he was checking directions, or a pastry had caught his eye? But she didn't believe in coincidence.

Her breathing started to falter. His presence was overpowering, demanding acknowledgment. She glanced up and saw his reflection in the window. He was looking straight at her, right into her eyes, his own wide with disbelief. A rush of desire pounded through her body as he stepped toward her, arms open. She turned and pressed her body into his.

He circled her with his arms. 'How the hell?' he asked. He put his hand under her chin and kissed her. She returned the kiss, sliding her arms inside his jacket.

He took her face in his hands. 'I've been so worried about you. I thought we'd lost you forever in the desert. How did you get here?' he asked.

'Long story.' She touched his face. 'I can't believe you recognised me so quickly.'

He leant his forehead on hers, circling her waist with his arms. 'I would know you anywhere. The way you walk. The tilt of your head.'

Anxiety started circling within her, screaming like a caged bird. If he could see her so easily, that meant others could look past the outer shell and see the person below. She pulled her thoughts back. A lack of confidence would always lead to quick detection. Sam was the anomaly, not the rule – her disguises had served her in the past, and they would continue to keep her safe in the future.

She glanced at the crowd slowing and pushing around them and remembered the woman on crutches had mentioned a green-eyed man on the plane. A small spurt of panic shot through her. It was dangerous to be seen with Sam.

'We're drawing too much attention. My hotel isn't far from here,' she said.

He smiled and grabbed her hand for a moment. Her skin tingled at his touch and her pulse jumped. They separated and walked in silence, keeping their distance without touching or acknowledging each other. He kept glancing at her, as if worried she would vanish into thin air again. She felt the warmth of his gaze and dropped her head to hide the smile she couldn't contain.

They walked through the foyer of her hotel and entered the lift in silence, giving every appearance that they were strangers, but when they stepped inside her hotel room, all pretence was gone. He winked at her, and her pulse jumped as he pulled her into his arms. She pressed herself against the entire length of him, kissing him and running her hands through his hair. His hands travelled all over her body, causing her nerves to spark and jump. He kissed her neck, slowly moving downwards, and she started to moan as he lifted her onto the bed, leaning over to kiss her shoulders and neck. Mallory reached up and slid her arms over his shoulders. He covered her body with his, and the fire building in her leapt as they folded into each other. She slipped her hands under his shirt, running them up his sides, over his chest, discovering answering heat from his body. He stopped for a moment, peeling his shirt off and undoing his jeans. She placed her hands on his bare torso, her skin burning on contact with his, so that it was impossible to keep her hands still. She slid her hands onto his hips and then up his back and over his shoulders, before thrusting them into his hair and pulling his mouth to hers. He shuddered and pulled her closer. Mallory pushed him away and slipped her dress off. She wondered for a moment if they should slow down, but he pulled her naked body against his, kissing her again. His sensuous hands left burning trails all over her, finding tender places she hardly knew existed. He moved all over her body with his mouth, making her squirm and moan, until she pulled him into her and they rocked together as one.

Afterwards, they lay in each other's arms, smiling at each other in silence. She was amazed at how comfortable she felt with him, as if all of the time they had spent pretending they were not attracted to each other had never happened. He ran his finger down her cheek and traced the line of her jaw.

'When I heard you'd been compromised, I wanted to go back and look for you. I will always protect you if I can.' He kissed her hand. 'You know that, right?'

She nodded. 'How did you end up here?'

'Same reason as you. On the hunt for Jimmy the Cat.'

'Are you going to turn me in?' She snuggled closer. 'Because I know where to find my father. We could work together.'

His eyes flashed. 'I bloody should turn you in right now, you know.' He stroked the soft skin along the inside of her arm. 'You know what would happen to me if I worked with you, right?'

She grinned. 'Well, you just make sure you don't get caught!'

Sam frowned. 'How do you see that working out?'

She sat up and pulled on her dress. 'I'm positive my dad

is in Scotland.' She reached out and grabbed his hand. 'We could go to France today. Catch the ferry from Zeebrugge. You tell your cronies you have intel on Jimmy that links him to Scotland.'

Sam watched her, his expression guarded.

'Come on! Everyone is talking about Scotland. It's only a matter of time till Jimmy ends up there.' She rolled her eyes. 'He's probably already on his way!'

He ran a hand over his forehead and sighed. 'There hasn't been any intel on our side about Scotland.'

She snorted. 'You wouldn't tell me if you had intel. Anyway, you guys only find out things when we want you to.'

He raised an eyebrow.

She held up a placating hand. 'Okay, sometimes we're careless, but honestly – most of you can't find your way home without directions.'

He eyed her for a moment, then launched, grabbing her before she could wriggle free. 'Perhaps you're right,' he said. 'But I do know how to stop you from making harsh judgements about the law.' He locked her in his arms and rained light kisses on her neck and shoulders until she giggled out loud. Then his kisses changed and her giggles stopped. They kissed again, their hands exploring each other again.

'I can't get enough of you,' he panted.

She held his gaze, looking deep into his eyes. 'I feel exactly the same,' she whispered.

They stared into each other's eyes as they made love the second time, both feeling the deepening connection developing between them. When they were done, they lay locked in embrace until she asked, 'What are you going to do?'

He hugged her to him. 'I'll worry about it tomorrow. You'll be the first to know.'

She smiled and kissed him. 'I'm not sure that's good forward planning, but I'll allow it because it's you.' She rolled over and lifted the hotel phone. 'You hungry?' she asked, and ordered food and coffee.

~

Mallory woke and checked her watch. She stared through the crack in the curtains. Darkness blanketed the city. If she were quick, she would be able to make the night train to Brussels, and then jump on the train to London. She gave herself a mental kick for mentioning the ferry to Scotland. That plan was out the window now. She would have to take the Eurostar and face her fear of the tunnel.

She watched Sam sleeping. His breathing was deep and steady, his face relaxed. She resisted the urge to kiss him, gently unwinding his arms from hers instead, and offered a silent apology for slipping the ground-up sleeping tablets into his coffee earlier that night. She'd known as she slipped the drug into his mug that she loved him, but she also knew she couldn't trust him to make the right decision for her. His love for her would always come second.

She rolled off the bed and started to move around the darkened room, packing her bag in silence, holding her breath for a moment when Sam rolled over, then waited until his breathing levelled. She needed enough time to get away, to throw him off her trail. It wouldn't matter if he tracked her to Scotland – the important thing was getting a head start. She had to get to the United Kingdom and through border control before he woke up and realised she had given him the slip, because he would raise the alarm with Interpol, for sure. If he wanted to find her, he'd have no choice. He would have to follow her.

Mallory stopped in front of the desk in the hotel lobby, smiling at the bored concierge who tried to stifle a yawn as she approached.

'Hi,' she said. 'My husband arrived in Bruges late last night. He's awfully tired and needs a good sleep. Can you please make sure he isn't disturbed?' She handed the concierge her key, and a tip. 'Can I fix the bill up now, please? I'm happy to pay for another night, but we will be out of the room by this afternoon.'

He nodded, a large smile appearing on his face. 'Where is your next stop after Bruges?'

She smiled, making sure she looked sufficiently distracted. 'We haven't decided. We're having a second honeymoon.' She flashed a shy smile and looked at the floor.

He noticed her bag on her back and frowned. 'Does Madam want to leave her luggage here?'

She shook her head. 'No, this is my daypack. I intend to do some exploring.'

'Do you need any information or maps?'

'No, thanks. I've done my research.'

He shrugged, losing interest when there was no prospect of another tip.

Mallory stepped into the quiet, chilly streets. Her breath steamed in front of her, and she felt the coldness of the pavement seeping into the soles of her boots. She shook her head, aware that it wasn't as cold as she felt. Living in the

Australian desert for over a year had made her soft. She stamped her feet and started toward the train station. Birdsong drifted above the street, the soft, musical calls so different to the raucous cries of the birds she had become accustomed to in the desert. Rays of morning sun touched the rooftops of the city, and she found herself comparing the weak light to mornings at the gorge. She stopped her thoughts, aware that she was becoming nostalgic.

The city was starting to come alive, and Mallory smiled, breathing in the buzz and energy. She stood on a corner, waiting to cross, enjoying the warmth from the vehicles waiting at the traffic lights. The last of the darkness lifted away, revealing a Dresden-blue sky. She stared up at the sight with a sudden rush of optimism. As she crossed the road to enter the station, the calm certainty that she was drawing nearer to her father enveloped her. Her path was clear: she would see him again.

5

MALLORY sank into the seat on the train and shoved her bag under the seat in front of her. The odour of sour coffee and stale food permeated the carriage, along with a faint undertone of tobacco. Her empty stomach turned, and the calmness she had felt in Bruges dissipated. In its place, a vague anxiety gnawed at her, its origin not entirely clear. She tried to quell it, even though she suspected it was probably the fact that she had to travel under the ocean to get to Britain. But there were so many things she could be anxious about that it seemed pointless to worry about anything. There was nothing she could do now, and not much to see until the Eurostar reached London. With any luck, Sam would not be disturbed and would sleep until lunch time, giving her at least a six-hour lead before he put the Heat onto her. Despite her lingering anxiety, she felt certain she would find her father if she made it to Scotland. Her only goal was to find him, but she just couldn't picture their reunion. No matter how hard she tried, the image she wanted to conjure wouldn't hold. She wasn't sure what she would do, or where she would end up after she found him.

The train moved in swift silence toward the tunnel. It was marvellous and frightening to think that she would soon be in that tunnel with an entire ocean pushing and heaving above. She felt her chest constrict and her anxiety flip, and pulled her thoughts away from the fact that she would be trapped under tonnes of water in a man-made tunnel, inside a vehicle that was clearly not waterproof. Getting into a panic wouldn't change the situation. Beads of sweat had popped up on her top lip at the thought.

She rubbed the sweat off her face, and forced herself to concentrate on the tourist pamphlets she'd picked up in Paris. She flicked through them, studying the rail system in England. She had already decided to change trains as soon as she reached London. It was better to start the final leg of the journey to Scotland immediately – the chances of reaching her destination without being intercepted were better if she kept moving. The easy part was getting to Edinburgh. Once there, she had to find the man, Petey, which would be no easy feat. No doubt the word was already out about Trafford. The Scots weren't likely to put any trust in her contacts, and the growing number of people who seemed to think she was connected to Jimmy the Cat alarmed her.

The meeting with Linus returned to her. She thought about his comments regarding Jimmy the Cat, and Ricky's veiled threats about Jimmy and her father's connections. She couldn't understand why everyone kept implying that her father and Jimmy were connected in a partnership of some kind, but the implications for her own safety were very clear. Jimmy was hated throughout her community, and there was the bad press Derek had created when he went down. The only people who were hated more than Jimmy the Cat were those who had shopped others to the Heat, and thanks to Derek, she was now on that list. She had enough enemies without adding all of Jimmy's to her list of threats.

The train slowed as it approached St. Pancras station. Mallory stretched her legs and took her time getting her belongings together. When the train stopped, she moved toward the door, looking like any other exhausted tourist. She stopped before approaching customs, pretending to make adjustments to her backpack. She wondered if Sam would tell Interpol about her presence in Europe. Whether he did or not, she didn't doubt that he would follow her. She checked her watch. If her calculations were wrong, and he was already awake, he may have already raised the alarm, and it may all be too late. She knew she had no other option but to attempt to get through border control. Hopefully, time was on her side. She waited in line at customs, passport in hand, shifting from one foot to the other and wincing every so often, as though her joints pained her.

When she reached the customs officer, he gave her a sympathetic smile. 'How are we today?'

'Tired and in need of a bed,' she said.

He glanced at her face and back to her passport. 'Is that an American accent I hear?' he asked, his expression bland.

Mallory smiled. 'Canadian, but I have dual citizenship. My father is Australian.'

The officer ran his eyes over her face and studied the passport again. 'Lucky for some, Miss.' He stamped it and handed it to her. 'Enjoy your time in London.'

She nodded, careful to keep her breathing regular and

her elation under control. She walked through the security gates toward Kings Cross Station and bought a one-way ticket, unable to contain her shivering excitement as she boarded the train to Edinburgh. Nothing could stop her now. The meeting with her father was getting closer, which meant she would finally have the answers she'd always craved. Mallory settled into a seat at the back of the carriage, pulled a pen out of her bag and spread a map of Scotland across her lap.

~

On the platform opposite, Jimmy the Cat watched Mallory board and take her seat on the train to Edinburgh. His eyes narrowed as he lit a cigarette and took a deep, appreciative drag. The train pulled out of the station and he grinned without humour at the empty space where it had been. A security guard approached and he casually flicked his cigarette away. The cigarette pinwheeled across the platform, leaving a trail of skittering sparks before it dropped over the edge onto the tracks.

The guard stopped beside him. 'Excuse me, Sir?'

Jimmy turned and studied the young man. He was no more than twenty-five. Tall, but soft around the edges with a flaccid chin, pale blue eyes and ginger hair already receding. A weak creature, relying on the uniform he wore to supply the gravitas he lacked.

Jimmy smiled and the guard recoiled involuntarily. 'Just keep walking, son. You're doing a fine job for Queen and country,' Jimmy said in a clipped, public-school accent.

The guard hesitated and Jimmy's smile disappeared. His arms dropped into the deep pockets of his coat, loose and at the ready.

'I can make all of the problems you've ever had in your short, futile life go away, son.' Jimmy looked the guard up and down, his lip curled into a sneer. 'Is that what you really want? A quick end to your sorry existence?'

The young man backed away without speaking, his hand on his radio.

Jimmy took a step toward him. 'Boo!'

The guard jumped, his face turning pasty white under a sheen of sweat. He started to unclip the radio on his belt with shaking hands.

Jimmy chuckled mirthlessly and lifted a hand, pointing his pocket at the man. 'Don't do that now, little big man. Just walk away and live to tell the tall tale at the pub tonight.'

The young man turned and scurried away. Jimmy pulled a ticket out of his pocket, the altercation already forgotten. He checked the platform numbers and strode toward the Glasgow train. Once boarded, he sat by a window, grinning like a schoolboy as the train pulled out of the station. He pressed his narrow face against the window, watching until the underground finally opened to grey skies and terraced houses. He drank it all in as the terraced houses gave way to country homes, green countryside, and villages of thatched roofs and whitewashed buildings nestled at the base of rolling hills.

An attendant stopped in front of his seat, and he passed his ticket to her. She glanced at the paper and returned it with a smile. 'Thank you, Sir. Enjoy your journey.'

'Nae fear, lassie,' he said in a broad Scottish accent.

As the train moved north, the country moved through imperceptible changes, and he smiled at the passing vista, noticing that the rhythm of the wheels seemed to echo his own thoughts, *I'm going home, going home, going home.* It had been far too long, but this time tomorrow he would be back in the Scottish Highlands. The thought of the glens and mountains of his childhood sent a shiver of excitement through him. Would the bothy of his childhood still be there? He hoped it would be just as he remembered it: the single room with an open fireplace, wood stove, scrubbed wooden table and narrow cots, surrounded by thick stone walls and covered by a heavy, thatched roof, all designed to keep the cold at bay.

The image brought back memories of deep winter, when the livestock were brought in to sleep the night in a narrow room along one side of the bothy. The scent of wet wool and feathers, and the sounds of chickens clucking and the milking cow scraping her horns on the walls were the night-time winter symphony of his childhood. He didn't regret the lack of running water; the near starvation and thick peat smoke in winter; the wild spring days spent in the forest picking mushrooms and hunting deer; the silent peaceful hours fishing on the loch; the regular beatings by his old man and brother – every experience had made him into a man. He bared his teeth at his reflection in the window. He had a family reunion to attend.

~

Mallory jumped onto the platform in Edinburgh station, scanning the area until she located the luggage lockers. She walked along the bank of metal boxes to the number Petey had told her to use. She stopped for a moment, as if considering her choice, while she scanned the nearby areas for surveillance. A group of young girls walked past, bantering back-and-forth in an accent unintelligible to her.

It did not sound like any English she had heard before. As she punched in the code and flipped open the door, she wondered if she would be able to understand anyone in Scotland. The locker appeared empty and her heart lurched. Was the whole thing a setup? Her senses were on red alert, but she kept her head down and her body relaxed, glancing either side, listening for approaching footsteps. She inspected the locker one last time. As her eyes adjusted to the dim interior, she saw a slim, beige wallet at the back of the locker, almost an identical shade to the shelf. She dumped her bag on the inside lip of the locker and slipped the wallet inside the front pocket, then she stood with her forehead resting against the cool metal above the open locker door, as if exhausted after a long journey.

The crowd continued to flow past her, and her adrenaline subsided. She closed the locker and walked away from the luggage stands toward the exit. When she stopped to get her bearings, a phalanx of Scottish matrons marched toward her, their tartan jackets and woollen skirts offering no quarter to obstacles. It was obvious they had no intention of easing their momentum or breaking their group for annoying tourists. She didn't want to cause a scene and stepped sideways as they swept past her, before following them along the platform and out of the station.

She stopped and stared at the vista before her. Edinburgh bustled and sighed, reminding her so much of a charming lady of standing, nose perfectly powdered, gloved, dressed in her Sunday best and enunciating every vowel, that Mallory couldn't resist a smile. She wandered along the street, enjoying the mix of accents floating on the crisp, midday air. She knew she should check the wallet for a meeting point as soon as possible, but she wanted to distance herself from the lockers, and it was never a good idea to rush anything.

She decided to tick off an item on her bucket list and visit the Ross Fountain. As she walked, she noticed the famous Edinburgh smell permeating the air; it reminded her of her childhood breakfast ritual of Weetabix and warm milk. She inhaled the scent, remembering the many stories her father had told her about Scotland. He always had a deep fascination with the country. She remembered him saying that the gardens containing the Ross Fountain were built after a loch, that defended Edinburgh Castle, was drained. She wandered along Princes Street, aware of the castle looming above the city, and turned into the gardens. The fountain was imposing but overshadowed by the castle above. She stood for a while, caught in the memories of her father. She studied the fountain, her eyes narrowing. The level of detail he'd given her about it was astounding – a person would have to visit more than once to know so much. She frowned, hit by the sudden realisation that she had never thought about the possibility of a Scottish connection before. Her father had an English accent, and had never visited Scotland when he was with her mother, but it was obvious to her now that there had to be some kind of personal connection. She glanced around at the crowds meandering around the fountain. Was it an old connection that had brought him back to Scotland now?

Mallory sat down on a bench in the park and pulled the wallet out of her backpack. She flicked a finger across the twenty-pound notes and pulled out a folded piece of card from behind the money, nodding in satisfaction. Petey had come through after all. She had a meeting point, and the possibility of help. She memorised the address on the card, then tore it into pieces and dropped them in a bin as she left the gardens and towards Old Town.

The walk to the meeting place, The Hanging Bat, was uneventful, but she remained alert and watchful. When she reached the bar, she scanned the surrounding streets but couldn't see any immediate threats. All the same, she wandered past the doorway, crossed Lothian Road and entered a Subway outlet, dropping her bag on a seat in the window of the store, before buying an iced tea and settling down to watch the bar across the road. She waited thirty minutes, observing as a couple came out of the bar and clung to each other in a swaying embrace before parting. A young woman entered the bar alone, and a middle-aged man in a kilt staggered onto the street, shaking his fist and yelling unintelligible insults at the staff within. He wandered toward the city, stopping for a moment to harangue a light pole. At the end of his soliloquy, he attempted a flying drop kick and landed in a heap without touching the pole in question. He lay on his back roaring obscenities at the sky, arms and legs flailing like a dying cockroach as he tried to regain his feet. Mallory grinned at his theatrics and turned back to her surveillance. There was no discernible threat near the bar. She checked her watch and slung the bag over her shoulder. It was time to move.

She crossed the street, stepped into The Hanging Bat and glanced around. The bar downstairs was empty, except for a couple with stony expressions, beers clutched in hands, and bodies slightly turned away from each other. The only other person in the lower bar was the bartender.

He nodded in her direction as he polished a glass. 'If you don't fancy a seat down here, there's more upstairs, lass.' He glanced at the couple, his meaning quite clear.

The tension that had been building in her eased. She ordered a beer, watching the couple out of the corner of her eye while the bartender served her. As she slid onto her stool, the man turned and smiled in her direction.

'Aye, that's alright, is it?' asked the woman, her voice dripping with bitter sarcasm. 'You're happy to smile at wee lassies, but you cannae take care of your own for love or money.'

'Orright hen, I see your point and all, but there's nae point smiling at you today now is there?' the man replied in an equally sarcastic tone. He shrugged. 'Aye, I'm just being friendly, is all.'

The woman stood up, knocking her stool over in the process. 'Friendly? Friendly? Is that what you call it, Gordie?' She pointed at him, her drink sloshing onto her hand and dripping onto the bar. 'Friendly like you were with that wee lassie in Dunoon? Are we talking that kinda friendly?'

The man slammed his glass down. 'That were fifteen years ago, hen. You weren't going with me at the time – I've nothing to be ashamed or feart about.'

The woman glared at Mallory. 'You hear that, lass? He's got nothing orright.'

Mallory kept her eyes on her drink. It seemed to her that the couple were less than a drink away from a major fight, and she didn't want to get involved. She hoped they would hold off until she had finished her business, because the last thing she needed was the police turning up. She slipped off the stool without acknowledging their conversation and walked up the stairs, placing her beer on a table and removing her jacket as she scanned the room. To the left of her was a nook. The young woman who had entered the bar earlier sat against the wall. Mallory made eye contact and the woman gave a slight nod. Mallory looked around the upper level. There was nobody else there. She spotted a fire exit on the back wall and her tension dropped a notch. She sat down near the woman, taking care to keep the steps leading to the room in her line of vision.

The other woman stared at the empty stairs and sipped her drink. 'First time in Edinburgh?' she asked.

Mallory nodded. 'Yes, it's really lovely.' She waited. It was hard to tell if the woman was her contact, or simply a local who was bored and wanted to chat with a tourist.

'You're older than I thought you'd be. I was expecting a wee lassie, maybe just graduated from training wheels.'

Mallory shrugged. 'You're more feminine that I thought you'd be.'

The other woman laughed. 'Aye well, Petey can't meet you. He sends his condolences.'

A shiver of apprehension passed through Mallory, making the hairs on her arms and neck stand up. 'Why?'

'Everyone knows why you're here, hen. There's none that can, or will, help you now.'

Mallory's apprehension deepened. She kept an eye on the stairs, aware that, despite the care she had taken, she may have walked into a trap. 'Then why meet me?'

'Steady lass, I mean you no harm.' She placed her drink on the coaster. 'Your old man still has some allies — few and far between — but they're out there.'

She turned and stared directly at Mallory for the first time, a frown marring her smooth forehead. 'You're not what I expected, hen.' She studied Mallory for a moment, as though weighing up her options. 'I was sent with a message. You'll not be finding Warwick Cash on the east coast.' She picked up her drink, studying the remains with a critical eye before draining the glass. 'If it's him you're wanting, you'll be needing to find the sanctuary between the mountains and the island sky.'

'What does that mean?'

The woman shrugged. 'Well now, I heard you are a clever one. You will have to work it out.' She stood and moved around the table, stopping to look Mallory in the eye, her gaze still full of sympathy. 'Take care, hen. You've enemies everywhere, including here, and some be from unexpected quarters.'

Mallory finished her beer and pondered the woman's riddle. She had two problems to contend with now. A stale disguise that was already compromised, and decoding a riddle to find her father somewhere in Scotland. She couldn't immediately work out what "the sanctuary between the mountains and the island sky" meant, but at least she knew she wouldn't find it on the east coast.

~

Sam watched foaming spray slam into the thick glass of the ferry window. Bubbles rolled across the glass, distorting his view of the towering waves heaving and crashing around the vessel. The sea was as wild, unfettered and equally as dark as his thoughts. He was disappointed with Mallory, but not entirely surprised. Once again, circumstances had shown him that there could be no real future for them. She would always choose the other side of the law. His chest constricted at the thought. He felt the weight of the connection between them – there was no denying his feelings, but Mallory was a career criminal. He couldn't compromise all of the years he'd spent building his own career, upholding laws he believed in, ensuring law-breaking individuals were brought to justice, just because he'd fallen in love with the wrong woman.

A flush of embarrassment and frustration passed through him. He had known that morning, even before he arrived in Zeebrugge with the Interpol operatives to apprehend Mallory, that she wouldn't be on the ferry. He had also known that they didn't believe his story about an unknown informer. The fact that they didn't take him in for questioning assured him, at least, that he had not been followed or observed when he met her yesterday. If they had seen him with Mallory in front of the bakery, they would have easily put the pieces of the puzzle together. He was on dangerous ground, and his feelings for her were the reason. They were clouding his judgment. He should have taken her in as soon as he saw her in Bruges, instead of giving in to his desire for her.

Fragments of the night they spent together in Bruges returned. He had wondered more than once if Mallory's mention of Scotland that night was nothing more than a red herring, but he trusted his instinct. She'd been truthful in that moment, convinced the authorities knew nothing about the possibility of her father's presence in Scotland, and equally eager to take him with her. A wave slammed into the side of the ferry with such ferocity the impact felt almost personal. He flinched, staring at the continuous wall of waves rearing up outside, and turned Mallory's words over in his mind. There was no doubt her guard was down when she shared that information; her derision at the blindness of lawmakers was palpable, as was her excitement about the possibility of finding her father. Yes, she may have chosen a different way to get to her destination, but he knew his best hope of finding her still lay in Scotland.

His thoughts returned to his earlier meeting with the French Interpol operatives, and he felt another stab of anxiety. The details he gave them were vague. He was surprised they hadn't pressed him for more. There was still a chance he was wrong, that they had been tracking him and were already aware of Mallory's disguise and the fact that he was compromised. He glanced at the passengers in surrounding seats, but no one appeared to be paying any attention to him.

Sam checked his watch. Two more hours and the ferry would dock. It was imperative to get to Scotland, catch Jimmy Contanti, and hopefully bring Mallory back in from the cold before too many players became involved. And if he did manage to bring her in? What then? The thought stalled him. The super would have no sympathy for her position now. He would terminate the safe house arrangement, and she would end up in jail with no protection. His chest tightened as the internal war between his ethics and his love for Mallory intensified. He stared at the heaving sea outside the window once more, acutely aware of how far he was from his country. The musty air in the ferry made him feel tired and overwhelmed, homesick for the endless, red-hazed horizon and pressing heat of the outback country he loved best. He could think out there, make reasoned decisions without the weight of other considerations clouding his vision. He turned his thoughts forward and leant back into his seat, determined to get some sleep before he reached Scotland. The race to catch Mallory and her father, and possibly retrieve the Topaz Stallion, would begin when he got there.

Sam woke to the sound of the ferry horn. He stretched and stared, disoriented, around the cabin until full consciousness returned. He looked out the window and saw a mix of villages and industrial areas crowding the banks along the Firth of Forth. As the ferry started to slow on its approach to the Forth Bridge and turn toward the Rosyth docks, he grabbed his bag, his thoughts already on his upcoming meeting with an agent from Scotland Yard.

~

Mallory studied the far north and West Coast regions of Scotland on a computer screen in Edinburgh Central Library. She magnified the Orkney Islands and read about the extensive mountain range, searching for any mention of a sanctuary between mountains and island sky, but no logical explanation presented itself. There didn't seem to be any way that a sanctuary could exist between the mountains and the sky on the islands near the northern Scottish coastline. She ran a hand across her forehead and tried to quell her growing frustration. The answer would no doubt be simple, as most riddles were. She rolled the map across the screen, bringing the West Coast into view. It was remote, sparsely populated – not the kind of place she'd imagined her father residing. He was a man who had always liked to be in the centre of things, a social creature who preferred crowds and attention, not one to retire to the safety of rural isolation even if he were laying low. If he had chosen such a path, the stakes must be very high indeed. Mallory hesitated. Was it possible he'd been hiding all of these years because of the Topaz Stallion? Or had he broken one of the unwritten rules and betrayed a comrade to the law? She pushed the thoughts away. She couldn't afford to focus on the dangers involved or she would freeze, and that was the most dangerous state of all.

She rolled the mouse south, following the line of the West Coast until she found the islands of Lewis and North and South Uist. She clicked on each island in turn, stopping when she saw mention of a Sanctuary Sculpture on North Uist. She clicked open another tab and googled the sculpture, but her elation at finding a possible clue was short lived. There was nothing to link the statue, or its surrounds, to mountains or sky. She turned her attention to the Isle of Skye, studying the mountains and settlements. There was nothing to suggest a sanctuary there either, but perhaps there was something in the name. The longer she thought about it, the stronger the possibility became – a sanctuary between mountains and the Isle of Skye. She rolled across the West Coast near the island and clicked on the few villages dotted along the coast. When she clicked on Applecross, the Scots Gaelic name for the Applecross Peninsula, *A' Chomraich*, meaning "The Sanctuary", appeared. She scrolled through the information, barely containing her excitement when she read that the Applecross Peninsula was referred to by locals as the sanctuary between the mountains and the Isle of Skye. It was remote and seemed like the last place her father would choose to live, but it had to be the answer to the riddle.

She sat back to think. A plan was needed. While Mallory considered her options, she noticed the reflection of a person on the computer screen, a familiar-looking woman entering the library, her figure silhouetted in the doorway of the library. Mallory stopped scrolling, closed the other tabs she had opened, and rolled the screen back to the West Coast, and then back further, checking which roads led to the island. Then she kept rolling south, stopping finally on the Mull of Kintyre. She clicked on the tourist links on the page, opening another tab with a search Mull of Kintyre. She continued to open new sites on information on the surrounding area, and leant toward the screen, as if she were reading the tourist information with deep interest. Finally, she clicked on the original tab, cleared the search information and closed it, leaving the Mull of Kintyre tabs open. After a few minutes more of scrolling, she left the computer and wandered toward the outer doors of the library, slipping outside without looking back. She scanned the area surrounding the library and drifted toward a café, taking a seat inside that offered a clear view of the library entrance. Fifteen minutes later, the woman she had seen reflected in the computer screen appeared on the steps.

Mallory dropped her head and whispered to herself, 'And that's three.'

The young woman's hair was tucked under a cap. The cast was still on her arm, but she was no longer using crutches. She was the same woman who had spoken to Mallory on the plane and later interrupted her meal in Bruges. Mallory lifted her phone in front of her face, filming the woman as she bounced down the steps two at a time. The crutches had been a disguise. She was supremely fit and agile, dressed in muted greys that were designed to blend into the crowd. Mallory was struck again by the familiarity of the other woman's movements. She racked her brain, on the verge of pinpointing the data, but she still couldn't join the dots. She waited until the woman disappeared around the corner before leaving the café and walking toward the shopping precinct. She couldn't stay in the city. There was no hope of procuring a change of identification – the risk of recognition increased with every hour that passed. It was time to get a new look and get out of Edinburgh. Her mind turned back to the woman's presence in the city. It seemed likely she was a professional, but she wasn't with the law and didn't appear to be connected to Trafford. Who was she, and why was she tracking Mallory all over Europe?

~

The young woman at the cosmetics counter in John Lewis ran an eye up and down Mallory, and raised a judgemental eyebrow as she approached the counter.

Mallory grinned, ignoring the girl's obvious distaste. The hair dye she'd chosen was jet black, not suited to her current complexion. She knew she looked washed out and sickly, and her clothes were crumpled and nondescript.

She slid onto the stool in front of the mirror and smiled at the hostile girl. 'Hey, I have a fancy dress tonight and I want to try out a new look. Is it okay if I use your samples? I want to see if this makeup will work.'

The girl stopped chewing her gum for a moment. 'Fancy dress? You're nae going to Burns Night?'

Mallory shook her head and the girl stared at her in open contempt, then glanced around before shrugging. 'I'm supposed to show you, but—' A sigh escaped her, and the girl's eyes rolled toward the ceiling before coming to rest on Mallory's unmanicured fingernails.

'Well, keep a brush in your hand. If you see your boss coming, we'll pretend you're hard at work.'

The girl glanced at her one last time with undisguised boredom and lifted her own hand to admire her brightly polished nails.

Mallory's attention was already on the makeup palette on the counter. She didn't know how the "crutches woman" had managed to track her to Edinburgh, but she was going to make it hard for her, or anyone else, to find her so easily again. She thought about the passport in her backpack. It was the only one she had, and it was stale. She knew it would already be flagged with Interpol, but if she were asked for identification by local police and they had no reason for suspicion, it would probably pass. The problem was changing her look just enough to escape the woman tracking her, but not so much that the passport would look wrong. She considered the problem as she adjusted tones and highlights to create a new look. She glanced at the girl, relieved to see her staring into the middle distance, the brush resting in her limp hand, her mouth chewing gum with bovine satisfaction, completely unaware of the transformation taking place beside her.

Mallory completed the look she was creating and fluffed up her hair, letting the fringe fall over her eyes. She moved away from the counter while the girl still daydreamed and wandered into the women's clothing section, selecting a nondescript hiking jacket and a pair of trousers before blending into the flowing crowd. She drifted through the different departments across the store, stopping to run fabrics through her fingers or try on hats and sunglasses, like any other day shopper. When she finally stepped onto the escalator leading back to the street, she reached into her backpack, put on a cap and sunglasses and studied a map of Scotland on her phone.

An hour later, Mallory was clipping on her seatbelt and adjusting the seat and mirrors in her hire car. She glanced at the sat nav, ignoring the touch screen as she spread a paper map of Scotland across the passenger seat. She wouldn't use the electronic system in the car; it was too easy to see where she'd been, and where she might intend to go. She traced the route past Perth along the A9 to her first stop – Aviemore. She kept following the thin line on the map until she reached the Applecross Peninsula. It would be at least six hours before she arrived. Once there, she would have to work out how to find her father. Doubt assailed her for a moment. What if she drove all the way to the West Coast and couldn't find him? What if she had misunderstood the riddle? She shook her head and started the car. She had to start somewhere, and while she couldn't remember why Applecross seemed familiar, there was something from the past, an echo that created a faint sensation of comforting nostalgia. She chased the feeling for a moment, trying to pin down a memory, but there was nothing. She pushed her doubts away, the momentary nostalgia making her feel confident she was on the right track.

6

SAM walked into the Scottish headquarters, unsure how he would be received. He flicked on his phone and double-checked the name of the operative he was supposed to meet, frowning at a cryptic message from the super about Warwick Cash. There was every chance Interpol had reported his contact with Mallory, but he couldn't see how it would relate to her father. He pushed his phone into his pocket. He would worry about the repercussions with the super when he returned to Australia. Right now, he was intent on finding Mallory and Jimmy Contanti.

A door opened behind the counter and a tall, thin man in a dark suit nodded at Sam. 'My name is Jervis, and you'll be Sam Walker. Come in, lad.'

He gave Sam's hand a firm shake when he drew level, his dark eyes taking in every detail. Sam felt his tension ease. He was in good hands here. The man was all planes and angles – his mind probably as sharp as his appearance. The man nodded toward an interview room, and Sam's tension returned. If he were questioned about his encounter with Mallory, he wouldn't be able to lie. He followed in silence, unsure whether he would be leaving Edinburgh a free man.

Jervis slid into a seat on the opposite side of the metal

table with a closed laptop in the centre. Sam glanced at the laptop, taking in the faint blinking light on the side. He sat back in his chair, keeping his arms open and his body relaxed.

Jervis opened the laptop, typed in a password and swung it toward Sam. 'Easier and safer if you read the intel, lad. I'm here if you have questions.'

Sam scrolled through the document, his eyes widening. It seemed incomprehensible that Mallory was right, but here it was in black and white. Warwick Cash was believed to be living on the West Coast of Scotland, practically under the noses of the authorities.

He looked up at Jervis, 'Has this been verified?'

Jervis gave a slight, shrugging nod. 'Let's just say some of the information is not entirely new to us. We've always known there was some connection between Warwick Cash and Jimmy the Cat, but we weren't aware of what it entailed.' He raised an eyebrow. 'We are waiting on verification of this information, so we haven't tried to find Cash. We know Jimmy is on the move, and may already be in Glasgow. We are quietly hopeful he will lead us to Warwick.'

Sam continued to read the final pages of the document in silence. He knew Jervis was watching his reactions, and he was careful to keep his expression neutral when he'd finished. He clicked the laptop closed and pushed it toward the other man. 'Thank you. That puts a new perspective on the situation.'

Jervis nodded. 'It does indeed.' He stood up and started toward the door. 'Come meet the intel team. They can give you a full debrief. When you're finished, I'll take you to your hotel.' He stopped, as if struck by a sudden thought. 'Oh, you will be in Edinburgh for the night – you must join us for Burns Night.'

'Burns Night?'

Jervis smiled. 'Yes, no time like the present to find out about Scottish culture. It may come in handy in your travels.' He opened the door and stood to one side to let Sam pass. 'I'll swing by your hotel and pick you up at seven pm. We're having supper at the Royal Yacht Brittania, so dress accordingly.'

Sam hesitated. 'I didn't pack to socialise.'

Jervis ran an appraising eye over him. 'I'm sure I'll find a jacket and tie to suit.'

Sam nodded, careful to mask his wish to refuse the invitation. He wanted to retreat to his hotel and consider his next move. He felt scattered, unable to concentrate while Mallory was on her own and possibly in danger, but he could also see that his refusal to attend would cause offence, or worse, invite closer scrutiny of his movements in Europe.

Jervis smiled and offered a small salute before leading him to the intel room. He opened the door and announced his arrival. Six operatives paused and studied Sam, as though he were an exhibit in a trial.

He smiled and stepped over the threshold, ready for the grilling that would follow.

'Until later,' Jervis murmured before closing the door.

A woman with piercing black eyes and pale skin beckoned to Sam. 'Well met, Walker. I'm Catriona McDonald and this is Nick Allan.' She motioned to a chair opposite her desk. 'Take a seat and we'll fill you in on what we have so far.'

Three hours later, Sam walked toward his hotel with his

head full of the information from the intel team. He realised things moved differently in Europe – there were more boundaries, less open spaces to make things happen, but it still seemed to him that the team in Scotland, considering the intel at their disposal, were wilfully slow in acting. He pushed his personal misgivings aside and went back through the facts. One thing was certain: he would be heading to the West Coast tomorrow.

~

The traffic on the A9 was light, and Mallory made good time to Aviemore. She stopped in the village and grabbed a coffee at a local café, wandering the streets while she sipped the beverage, slowing her pace to admire the whitewashed walls and red trim on the cottages. The mountainous Cairngorms beyond the town reminded her of the Rockies. They were currently turning on a colourful winter glow, the oranges and reds contrasting beautifully with the lighter greens in the valleys. She could easily imagine them under snow. A deep pang of homesickness rippled through her, followed by the memory of the last time she'd been there. A surge of hot anger replaced that homesickness at the reminder of Derek's betrayal, followed by aching melancholy at the thought of Sam's presence in Canada and everything that had transpired afterwards. Her home in the Rockies belonged to another lifetime now. She finished her coffee and jumped into the car, gunning the engine as she left the village.

Mallory followed the empty road, her mind focused on the many possible outcomes of meeting her father, until a deer leapt across the road ahead. She slowed the car and checked the verges on either side. Inverness was over an hour behind her now. She was on the last leg to Applecross. The isolated road through the mountains was narrowing to one lane, with intermittent passing sections along the way. She glanced at her phone. There was no reception. It wouldn't do to have an accident up here. There was every chance she could sit on the road for a couple of days before another traveller came by. And if that traveller happened to be unfriendly, she would be all alone in the Highlands with no weapons.

The road seemed to go on forever, and then Applecross Peninsula appeared, as though it really were suspended between the sky and the mountains. She pulled over, enthralled by the virtually untouched beauty of the sweeping bay below. There was very little in the way of settlement along the coast. A few stone cottages with gabled roofs dotted the landscape, but her eye was drawn to a large mansion overlooking the bay, its noble lines white and stark amongst the greenery. A strange feeling of familiarity came over her, so strong she felt tears spring to her eyes. She searched her memories, but again came up blank. To the best of her knowledge, she had never been to Scotland in her life, and yet, she felt certain she had seen the building before. But that certainty had to be an impossibility.

She started the car and drove down into the bay, stopping at the Applecross Inn. A sharp, icy wind off the water cut through her t-shirt when she stepped out of the car. She grabbed her jacket and looked at the black storm clouds gathering over the sea, shivering involuntarily before stepping into the inn. The glow of an open fire bouncing off burnished wood offered an immediate cosy warmth, and the sting of the cold air outside faded from her cheeks. She ordered a pint and looked around the empty hotel, wondering what she should do next.

The outside door slammed open and a young man rushed through, fighting to close it against the wind. 'Ah now, there's a huge storm blowing in this afternoon, Jarrod,' he yelled at the bartender.

'Aye man, no need to blow a gasket when we've company,' the bartender grinned and nodded his head toward Mallory.

The young man reddened and smiled vaguely at Mallory. 'Afternoon, lass. We've a mighty storm coming in. You'll not be wanting to travel further tonight.'

She smiled at the bartender. 'Well then, I hope there's a room available in this lovely establishment.'

He winked. 'Despite the crowds of incomers overrunning the place, we're not booked out just now.'

Mallory looked around at the empty bar and laughed. She ordered a drink, choosing a table close to the fire to spread her map out, lifting her glass to the bartender in appreciation as soft music started to hum through the warmth of the nook.

The young man collected his drink and approached her table. He hesitated a moment, then thrust out a hand. 'The name's Gregor, Miss.'

'Samantha.' She shook his hand as he dropped into the seat across the table.

'What brings you to Applecross?' he asked.

'I'm a photographer. Nature, wildlife. I love out-of-the-way places.'

He nodded. 'Aye well, you've come to the right place and all, then.' He leant back for a moment, studying her. 'If you're around tomorrow, you should visit the Flower Tunnel. It's a bit out of the ordinary. A polytunnel greenhouse down on the bay, with a wood-fired pizza restaurant inside.'

She looked at him, her doubt obvious.

'Aye lass,' said the bartender. 'That is real and all.'

Gregor nodded. 'There's plenty to see around here if you know where to look. There are some Highland families up here that would be happy to see you in a bothy, if you want to spend some time in the wild, too.'

'Bothy?'

He nodded. 'They're huts to bunk in while you're away in the Highlands.' He studied her a moment, then winked. 'I can always keep you company if you're afraid of the dark.'

Mallory shook her head, her expression neutral. 'The dark doesn't confront me.'

He smiled. 'Honest, you dinnae look like you're bothered by much, lass.' He glanced at the map on the table. 'It's a shame we're not having a proper Burns Night here tonight, but if you're wanting a true Scottish experience, you should away to Plockton tomorrow night. There's a Ceilidh on.'

'Ceilidh?'

He grinned. 'You've not done much research and all, then.'

Mallory noticed that his smile didn't reach his eyes and that his tone was suddenly wary.

She smiled with as much warmth as possible and leant forward to touch his hand. 'Well, you're right there, Gregor. I came to the West Coast on a whim. I heard about Lochcarron and wanted to see where tartan is made.' She sat back, relieved when he relaxed and raised his glass to her.

'We'll see you right, then. A Ceilidh is a traditional dance. You'll love it if you're of a mind to join in. And you'll meet plenty of interesting types there.' He laughed. 'Aye, there'll be some Highlanders and more at the dance for sure. Distance is nae barrier to a Ceilidh.'

Mallory's interest was piqued. She wasn't sure how, but there had to be someone or something at a local gathering that would point her in the direction of her father. The Ceilidh would be the perfect place to start.

She nodded in agreement. 'That sounds really interesting. I'll keep it in mind.'

Gregor grinned, a red flush creeping up his face as he raised his glass. 'Aye, you do that. Will you be joining us for a small supper to mark Burns Night tonight?'

She shook her head. 'I've had a long drive. I need to sleep.' She finished her drink and said her goodbyes as she stood. She knew how dangerous gossip could be in small communities. It was best to avoid prolonged conversations.

Later in her room, she lay on the bed and thought about finding her father. She stared at the ceiling, dropping into a meditative state, allowing images of him to return; his red hair and manicured beard, the glass that was never far from his hand. She frowned at the sudden image, the memory of clinking ice and the overpowering scent of single malt whiskey. Was he an alcoholic? That was not how she remembered him. He was always laughing, telling jokes, making her mother giggle. That much she did remember. And always so immaculately dressed in silk shirts and elegant suit jackets. A sudden memory flashed, of her mother and father fighting about the cost of a coat. She remembered the coat vividly. Camel-hide with wool lapels, perfect stitching and large wooden buttons with intricate engravings.

He'd shrugged it over a freshly laundered forest-green silk shirt, and yelled, 'I bring in the coin, hen! What do you bring? Nothing but bairns, boredom and bleating.' He stomped outside, leaving deep prints in the snow as he marched toward a sleek black car at the end of the drive, the motor already running.

Her mother had watched in silence, tears running down her cheeks and soaking into the neckline of her faded woollen cardigan. When she slumped onto the wooden chair, she had drawn her daughter into her arms. The pinching hunger the memory evoked, a hunger she had in fact felt through most of her childhood, returned to her. Mallory turned the echoes of the memory over, her thoughts confused. There it was again – a memory that didn't seem to belong to her history. This was not a childhood she remembered. Hers was one of abundance, warmth, laughter and love, a childhood where her parents were happy and loving, kissing each other often and hugging their children close. She frowned as another image returned of her mother sitting on a chair in a cold kitchen, sobbing into her hands while her father upended an almost empty whiskey bottle into a tumbler.

'How can you drink when we've no wood for the stove?' her mother cried.

Her father had laughed as the last of the fluid drained out and he dropped the empty bottle into the sink, but there had been no mirth in the sound.

Another night returned, and once again she recalled the

gurgle of an emptying bottle and clink of ice, but this time the crash of breaking glass followed.

Her brother had grabbed her hand in the darkness of the bedroom, and whispered, 'Don't go out there, Mally.'

She remembered shivering in the cold bedroom, and her brother's ribs digging into hers as he pulled her close under the thin blankets. She tensed further at the memory of his silent tears rolling down his cheeks and wetting her face as the sound of fists hitting flesh began.

Mallory sat up, her breathing ragged, her heart thumping. She felt her pulse thud threateningly in her temples and breathed deeply, willing calmness to return. She didn't understand where the memories had come from. She sifted through her prominent memories, focusing on the beautiful man with laughing golden eyes and hair like a burnished sunset, the man who lifted her in his arms as his rich laughter filled the house. The man who said kind words and conjured surprises out of his pockets like a magician.

The bleak memories she just witnessed could not be hers, but there was no doubt they were real; she could feel it. Mallory closed her eyes and thought hard about her father, remembering every detail: his broad smile and even white teeth, the way his long legs always spilled out of the recliner and filled the living room; the creases around his glowing eyes when he smiled, the narrow blackness in those same eyes when he was angry. His bouts of anger returned to her and she exhaled in shock. How had she forgotten the real truth of their situation? Forgotten how absent he was so much of the time, how angry he was most of the time when he was at home. How careful her mother was when he was there, always trying to placate him. The feeling of walking on eggshells returned. How had she forgotten how much room he took up in the house, the sheer dominating size of him blocking any recourse to argument? She shook her head. All marriages had bad times. It was obvious she had suppressed the bad memories. After all, she had wanted to preserve a perfect picture of her father, and that was normal, right? Doubt niggled at her. Did she really know her father at all? Would she recognise him if she met him? Would she even like the aggressive man she had just remembered?

She rolled off the bed and walked over to the window, watching the choppy water in the bay, its mood sullen in the gathering darkness below. She continued to wonder about her father. The memories had chased away the closeness and joy she had always felt when she thought of him, and made the possibility of finding him seem suddenly remote. She felt tears pricking at the back of her eyes. Perhaps she had set herself an impossible task. The West Coast was a vast area, and she realised now that she didn't even know the man she was looking for. He could be anywhere. He might not even be in Scotland.

She watched cormorants wheeling and diving along the shoreline as they chased their last meal from the depths before nightfall. Mallory wondered where her father was at that moment. Was he staring at the same sullen waters slapping at the coastline, listening to the cries of those same cormorants and thinking about her? It seemed unlikely, but she had no choice but to continue. Nothing would be gained by giving up now. She'd learned that persistence and observation could yield results when all else failed. All she could do was follow her instinct and keep searching. She turned away from the window, turned on the light and opened her map on the desk. The paper sluffed across the polished wooden surface as she smoothed out the fold lines, the sound barely audible over the gusts buffeting the window across the room. Mallory took in the heavy black clouds settling over the bay. She had a sudden urge to keep moving, but there was no point risking the storm. The local roads were bad enough in good weather.

She focused on the map. It was less than two hours to Plockton. She would go there in the morning, book a room and find out how to join the Ceilidh. It sounded like it would be a large gathering from the surrounding area. It would be a perfect opportunity to watch and listen, and at this point, it was the only obvious way forward. She felt doubt curling within her again, knotting her stomach and tangling her thoughts. The memories of the darker times of her childhood had thrown her. It was so long since she had seen her father. She pushed the map away and returned to the window. The last of the sunlight was gone, replaced by weak moonlight glowing intermittently through the heavy clouds. The heaving water below was barely visible, but she could hear the roar of the surf over the wind. She thought of Sam. The hairs on her arms lifted as goosebumps pimpled her skin. He felt suddenly close, as if he were standing beside her. She sighed and wondered if he were still in Europe, or if he had already made it to Scotland. Either way, she knew he wouldn't give up. Memories of the night in Bruges returned, but she quelled the feelings that rose in her chest. Her heart contracted painfully at the truth she'd yet to fully accept: Sam was one more obstacle she had to avoid if she wanted to find her father.

Sam watched the Rover roll to a halt in front of the hotel. The windows were so darkly tinted it was impossible to see who was in the car.

A rear window rolled down. 'Jump in, lad.' Jervis grinned and motioned to the other side of the car.

They pulled away, the driver navigating the traffic with smooth efficiency.

Jervis flicked a jacket and tie onto Sam's lap. 'I decided we'd be best to have a driver tonight. Aye, Burns Night can get a bit loose.' Jervis raised an eyebrow at Sam, the challenge unmistakeable.

Sam smiled as he slipped the tie under his collar and tightened the knot. 'I will be hitting the road early tomorrow, Sir. I will have to abstain.'

Jervis shrugged. 'You'll have to have one single malt, son. Would be criminal not to.' He glanced toward the driver and his voice dropped. 'What's the plan?'

Sam didn't want to reveal too much, although there was no reason to think Jervis and his team posed a threat. In fact, he knew the opposite were true, and it would be safer for him to let them know where he would be.

'I'll head to the West Coast and see what I can find out.'

Jervis nodded. 'We'll keep ears and eyes on the situation. If we think you need back up, we'll be sure to get some operatives over there.'

Sam nodded and glanced at the driver. 'What is this area of Edinburgh called?'

'We're in Leith, now,' said Jervis, before launching into a history of the area.

Sam leant back, relieved to have changed the subject.

He let the words roll over him, enjoying the information and the musical brogue of Jervis' voice until they came to a halt in front of the Royal Yacht Brittania.

He laughed as they walked toward the yacht, and admitted that he had expected a restaurant, not an actual yacht.

Jervis stopped, his eyes wide. 'But it's famous, man. I thought everyone knew about the Royal Yacht?'

Sam shook his head. 'My only defence is I am a long way from home, Sir.'

Jervis clapped a hand on his shoulder. 'Aye, and no doubt otherwise distracted?'

A jolt ran through Sam's body. He wondered what intel the other man had on his movements.

Jervis gave Sam an appraising look for a moment before continuing, 'Well, no matter. We'll treat you to a proper Scottish heels-up tonight, lad.'

As they boarded the Yacht, a group of men dressed in traditional kilts and carrying bagpipes approached Jervis.

'It's about time you showed your face, man,' boomed a gigantic, red-faced man with a huge grin. 'We're about to pipe in the guests!'

'Come now, you know I willnae be late for the pipes,' Jervis replied.

The group of men roared in approval and gathered Jervis into a group hug, while Sam smothered a smile at the change in the other man's accent and demeanour.

One of the men stepped away and thrust a hand out to Sam. 'I'm Thomas. I'll take a guess that you're nae from this part of the world, laddie?'

Sam shook his hand. 'You guessed right. Australia, mate.'

The man threw his head back and laughed. 'Lads, we've a live one from Downunder. We'll nae fall for his stories of drop bears, rabid kangaroos and monster crocs, just now!'

The group joined in and bellowed together, 'Aye lads! Let's show him how Burns Night is done right!'

The group turned as one and made their way along the corridor.

'You'll not find a more solid group of men, Walker,' Jervis remarked as they made their way to the bar and ordered drinks. A cluster of smartly dressed men and women approached, their curiosity about Jervis' companion apparent.

Sam nodded and made appropriate comments to each person Jervis introduced him to, taking note of those he felt would be important to remember. He nursed the whiskey Jervis had insisted he try, and glanced around the plush surroundings, only half-listening to stories about Burns Nights gone past and the life and times of the famous Scottish poet.

The musical wail of a bagpipe quietened the room, and he frowned in question at Jervis.

The other man smiled. 'There's nae reason to fear. They'll be here just now to pipe in the guests.'

The group of men who had greeted them in the corridor entered the bar area with bagpipes in full skirl. The crowd gathered and followed them toward the dining room. Sam stayed with Jervis, drifting with the crowd as the music swelled and wailed to a deafening level in the confined area. The excitement in the room permeated the atmosphere, and he grinned at the sight of the kilted pipers giving it their all ahead of the guests.

Sam took his seat in the dining room, aware that his ears were buzzing slightly as the sound of the pipes receded.

A grey-haired man in steel-rimmed glasses, ruffled shirt, kilt and sporran stood at the head of the room and tapped his champagne glass with a tiny spoon. 'Before we break bread, we've the Selkirk Grace to attend.'

The guests stood and Sam followed suit, keeping his eyes downward out of respect for the recital of the Grace.

"Some hae meat and canna eat,

And some wad eat that want it,

But we hae meat and we can eat,

Sae let the Lord be Thanket!"[i]

Sam raised his glass in toast and remained standing with the guests as waiters appeared with covered silver platters. The one remaining piper started to play and the man who had led the prayer started to recite a poem. Sam frowned at Jervis.

The older man leant toward him and whispered, 'It's the Address to the Haggis, lad. We'll nae sit until the finish.'

Sam nodded, his eyes on the unpalatable looking sausage-like food on the platters.

Jervis, as if reading his mind, gave a low chuckle. 'You'll nae go hungry, now. Haggis certainly tastes better than it looks. Add neeps and tatties, wash it down with good single malt, and you've been treated to a meal fit for the Gods.'

Sam watched, his interest piqued by the ceremony surrounding the meal.

After they were seated, he smiled at the older man. 'Are we okay to eat, or is there something more?' he asked. He didn't want to make a mistake and offend his host.

Jervis nodded. 'Aye, tuck into it, man. We'll be enjoying some of Burns' songs along the way – *Tam O'Shanter* and the like, and we'll be having the Toast to the Lassies and a vote of thanks.' He stopped speaking, grinning as the waiter dolloped food onto his plate. 'We'll finish with *Auld Lang Syne*, of course.'

Sam kept his face neutral as he lifted a forkful of Haggis to his mouth. He nodded in surprise at the taste.

Jervis laughed. 'Aye, it is better than it looks.'

The meal concluded, but the entertainment continued, with the crowd getting increasingly rowdy as more whiskey was consumed.

After the festivities finished and the driver was on their way, Sam assumed he had finished his cultural education for the night, but Jervis had other plans.

'We'll not take you back to the hotel yet, laddie. We've a Ceilidh to attend.'

Sam felt a deep fatigue wash over him, but he could also feel the other man's excitement and didn't want to offend, so he smiled in assent as he entered the vehicle.

When they reached the Ceilidh, Jervis leapt from the car and beckoned Sam to follow. The building looked like an old community hall, similar to ones in small towns in Australia, except it was stone instead of wood. He could see shadows flashing past the window and hear the high notes of fiddles and the shouts of revellers indoors. The door flung open, and the smell of whiskey, sweat and smoke drifted into the night. Sam grinned at the dancers whirling across the expanse of the wooden floor inside.

Jervis let out a whoop. 'This is a real Ceilidh, my man.

I'm hoping you can keep up,' he yelled, before flicking Sam a lazy salute and disappearing into the heave of dancers near the doorway.

Sam stepped back against the wall and watched with interest. The set moves of the dances reminded him of painful afternoons learning square dances in primary school. The anxiety of being overlooked, the horror of being chosen, the absolute shame of touching a girl in front of the entire class, the clear knowledge that she was hating the experience as much as he was – it all returned to him. He moved closer to the door, intent on slipping away before Jervis noticed.

A woman appeared, blocking his easy exit. 'Laddie!' she roared. 'The sidelines isnae the place for a fine specimen like yourself!' She grabbed his arm, her grip stronger than he expected, and dragged him into the milieu.

'Dinnae lose your feet, laddie. You'll nae see the light of day again if you do.' She laughed as she flung him toward the next dancer in the line.

Sam kept up with the pace of the dance and felt his mood lift as his body found the rhythm and his limbs released the tension he'd been holding. He shut out his worries and let himself go with the crowd until the music abated and the dancers dispersed toward the bar. He checked his watch and realised it was almost one in the morning. He caught Jervis' eye and offered a small goodbye wave, before slipping out the door into the chill quiet of the Edinburgh night.

He walked toward his hotel and noticed the famous Edinburgh smell that he'd read about was caused by a brewery on the edge of the city. He'd heard people complain about it on the ferry over, but it didn't seem that bad to him. The malty smell reminded him of the oatmeal, cream and brown sugar his mother always made him on a freezing winter morning. He was caught in the memory and stopped to look at the stars, so different to the ones he loved in the Southern Hemisphere. The streets were empty, almost deathly quiet, but as he neared the city centre, a crowd spilled out of a bar in front of him.

Cries of 'See you!' and the strains of *Auld Lang Syne* echoed off the stone walls of the buildings as they stumbled toward a waiting taxi. He grinned at their antics as he crossed the road and made his way to his hotel, but his mind was already on Mallory. Tomorrow he would be on his way to the West Coast. He would not rest until he tracked her down and brought Jimmy the Cat to justice.

7

WHEN Mallory entered the dining room for breakfast, Gregor was already sitting at a table, a plate loaded with toast and eggs in front of him. The smells wafting through the dining room made her stomach growl in appreciation.

He looked up as if he had heard the noise, and her cheeks flushed. He smiled, his cutlery poised above the impressive stack of food, then gestured with studied nonchalance to the chair opposite. 'We're the only ones here. Come join me, lass.'

Mallory felt a prickle of apprehension. His presence at the hotel for breakfast, his apparent casual demeanour. All of it seemed intentional.

She hung her jacket over the back of the chair before sitting and nodded at his plate. 'Are there any eggs left?'

He laughed, the sound deep and clear in the empty dining room. 'Aye. There's no shortage of food here.' He placed his cutlery on his plate with care. 'I'll not lie, I don't normally eat breakfast at the hotel.' His gaze dropped to the table, his own cheeks glowing cherry-red as he fiddled with his napkin. 'I decided to see you again, to ask if you'd be wanting a partner for the Ceilidh, perhaps?'

Mallory's anxiety eased. He was nothing more than a

young man, hoping for a date with a tourist. She studied him a moment longer. His sense of humour showed on his face and his eagerness to please was obvious. His nails were clean and his clothes were casual and tidy. He was a tall, solidly built and attractive young man, with strawberry blonde hair and a thick beard that were a perfect foil for deep, blue eyes. They would look good together. She imagined them, twirling and clapping with a crowd of dancers, their bodies pressed together when the music slowed, and immediately dismissed the idea. There was only one man she wanted to dance with now, and he wasn't an option. Besides, this man, Gregor, he would be known in Plockton. He would draw attention and insist on introducing her to the locals. He would want everyone to know that he was escorting the photographer from out of town, and would probably try to set her up with connections in the Highlands. He would try to build on their meeting and make it more than was warranted. He would mean well, but he would make it impossible for her to move freely, and no doubt endanger her in the end.

He looked up at her and she smiled and shook her head. 'Thank you so much for the offer. I have decided to keep exploring. I am going to Plockton, but I'm not sure if I'll get to the dance.'

He tried without success to hide his disappointment. 'Will you be coming back this way, do you think?'

She lifted her shoulders, the movement noncommittal. 'I'm not sure. It will depend on the scenery.'

He stared at her, his gaze suddenly appraising. 'It must be good and all, to have a job that allows so much freedom?'

She caught the mix of curiosity and suspicion in his

tone, and her guard returned. 'It may seem that way, but I assure you I am always chasing that perfect shot. I have deadlines and bills to pay, just like everyone else.' She paused for a moment and decided to deflect any more questions. 'If you don't mind me asking, what do you do for a living?'

He smiled. 'I work on a farm, lass. A mix of sheep and cattle.' He spooned three sugars into a black tea and continued. 'It's hard work, but I really enjoy working with livestock.' He looked up at her through his lashes. 'Aye, and it can get lonely and all.'

She smiled in agreement. 'Yes, I'll bet it can.'

He nodded and returned his attention to demolishing his breakfast. Mallory decided he had accepted her story and would not ask further questions, so she relaxed, happy to enjoy his company.

At the end of their breakfast, Gregor shook her hand and wished her safe travels. He held onto her fingers for longer than necessary, squeezing gently, his eyes warm with an unspoken invitation. Mallory felt a new wave of apprehension at his touch. She glanced around the dining room, noticing the small smiles and exchanged glances with the few staff on duty. She was drawing far too much interest. It would be best to leave this village as quickly as possible.

Later, as she drove along winding road toward Plockton, she couldn't help glancing in the rear-view mirror, but the road remained empty behind her. She smiled, her anxiety dropping a few levels, and returned her attention to the equally empty road in front. A herd of deer leapt across the road in the distance and she slowed automatically, taking in the surrounding countryside while she thought about her current situation. It was impossible to move through any community without leaving a trace, but small communities were the worst. Everyone watched; everyone had an opinion, and worst of all, everyone talked about their opinions at length to anyone that would listen. All the same, the tension she had been carrying since she arrived in Applecross was beginning to fade. Now that she was moving, she felt she would be able to stay ahead of the gossip. She knew it was more than possible to achieve what she wanted and still get the drop on everyone else in the game.

~

Sam hit the road before dawn, heading toward the West Coast. He considered the information he had received from Jervis and the intel team the day before. It seemed Warwick had remained free because Interpol had a bigger target in their sights – they had been holding off, waiting and hoping for the day Jimmy the Cat would make contact. He wondered if Mallory was aware of her father's past and her family relations. She had never mentioned that he was Scottish, or his connection to Jimmy. He glanced out the window at the still waters of yet another loch gliding by and considered the link between Jimmy and Warwick. His thoughts wandered back to Mallory, to their meeting in Bruges. An electric buzz ran through his body, but he dragged his thoughts away from the memory of her naked in his arms. The new information he had meant she was completely lost to him now. There was a strong possibility that she may be colluding with Warwick and Jimmy. He felt a visceral stab at the idea of her betraying his trust, but he pushed his feelings aside. He had to concentrate on tracking and apprehending Mallory and Jimmy. Bringing Warwick in from the cold would be an added bonus.

The sun was starting its afternoon descent when Sam pulled into the carpark of the hotel in Applecross. He shrugged on a jacket against the crisp breeze and left the car, heading across the road toward the bay, taking in every detail of the serene countryside and sparsely populated coastline as he walked. He stopped near the water and watched cormorants, seagulls and two birds he didn't recognise circling above the water. He kept walking and smiled when he spotted seals basking on the shores. He felt the tension of the past few weeks easing as he walked in the peaceful mid-afternoon silence. There was no threat here, and nothing to do except enjoy the strange country he found himself in. Cottages, like the one he'd seen in Aviemore when he stopped for coffee, were dotted along the opposite shore, and he could see a campsite further along the road. The country was beautiful, but foreign to his eye. He turned back toward the hotel, certain he would be able to get a fresh seafood lunch before his journey resumed.

He entered the hotel and stopped, waiting a moment for his eyes to adjust to the dark interior. The bartender looked up and smiled, his relief at the boredom of very few patrons apparent. Sam walked toward the bar and pulled out a stool as the bartender approached.

The young man nodded slightly and placed the glass he was polishing on a shelf under the bar. 'Hallo. Will you be wanting a drink and a bite to eat?'

Sam nodded. 'Beer please.' He looked around the bar. 'And seafood if it's not out of the question.'

The barman nodded. 'Seafood is our specialty. We'll see you right.' He grinned. 'What's the accent, then? You don't sound English, and an Englishman would never ask for beer without saying what type they'd be wanting.'

Sam smiled. 'I'm Australian.' He pointed at the taps near the till. 'I'll have a half of your Tennent's, thanks.'

The barman nodded, pulled the beer and handed it to Sam. 'Aye, good choice. I'll tell the kitchen to do scampi and chips. You'll know you've found heaven on a plate, pal.'

Sam raised his glass. 'Sounds good.'

The barman contemplated him for a moment. 'You here on business or doing a tour?'

Sam smiled. 'Holiday.'

'Well, you're the second incomer in as many days, now. It's a bit unusual for this time of year. Although we've not seen snow this season, so not impossible, I guess.' He dragged a tray of glasses closer to Sam and selected one to polish, his face pensive. 'Now there was a lass through here yesterday. A real beauty.' He shoved the cloth into the glass and scrunched it with vigour. 'A photographer – wildlife. She didn't say her nationality, but her accent sounded a little bit like yours. Perhaps she was from New Zealand, or a different part of Australia?'

Sam nodded as he lifted his drink, taking care to cover his interest. 'Wildlife photography is an interesting career choice.' He looked toward the windows at the front of the bar that faced the bay. 'She came to the right place. There'd be plenty of beautiful country around here to photograph.'

The bartender shrugged. 'Aye, you'd think. I'm certain my mate, Gregor, said she mentioned the Highlands. Aye, we told her about a Ceilidh in Plockton, but she was away early today in her little red car. I'm guessing the Highlands is more popular with world audiences than the coast.'

He placed the finished glass on the shelf and dropped his towel on the counter below the bar.

Sam nodded with a bored expression and turned his attention to the local paper, flicking it out to indicate he was finished with the conversation.

The bartender waited a moment and said, 'Anyway, I'll organise that meal for you.'

Sam kept his eyes down and nodded his thanks, his thoughts on Mallory. He hadn't expected to cross her trail so quickly, and now he had a place to start looking and the colour of the car she was driving. The mixture of elation and beer made him feel light-headed for a moment. He placed the beer on the bar. Now was not the time to get cocky.

His meal arrived and he tucked in, amazed at the freshness and taste of the seafood. The bartender moved up and down, cleaning and watching, ready to serve his only customer. Sam decided that when the time was right, he would try to find out what type of car Mallory was driving and which direction she had taken, but for now he would enjoy his meal and the quiet solitude of the empty bar.

A gust of wind slammed into the building, making it shudder and groan. Sam looked out the window and noticed the sky had turned black.

The bartender stopped beside him. 'There's a huge storm coming. Second one in two days. It's not a good idea to attempt driving up here in a winter storm.'

Sam glanced out the window as lightning lit up the waters on the bay. A rumble of thunder was followed by the sound of rain and a deepening darkness outside. 'What about that place, Plockton? Is it easy to reach?'

The bartender rubbed his chin. 'Aye, it's not too far, but you'll not get any help if anything goes wrong on the road there. There's none up here that will travel in storms.'

'The other tourist that was here, the photographer, did she risk the storm?'

The bartender shook his head, and Sam weighed up his options. It was better to stay here, get some much-needed rest, and start fresh in the morning. He knew that Mallory didn't have much of a head start on him. There was no guarantee that she intended to head toward the Highlands, and even if she did, there were plenty of places to hide, but it would be impossible for her to avoid any human contact, and that would be her undoing.

~

Three hours after she left Applecross, Mallory rolled into the village of Plockton. Well-kept, whitewashed buildings lined the main road into the village, their demure exteriors exuding an air of understated pride. Three men in caps stopped talking as she passed the village shop, their heads following the trajectory of her car until she slowed to a halt in front of the hotel. She watched them in the rear-view mirror, waiting until they lost interest and returned to their conversation. She ran an eye over the hotel. It looked quiet and traditional, but she decided to look for something more private, where there was less chance of prying local eyes and ears, or lonely young men who asked too many questions. She turned down a narrow side street, stopping in front of a bed and breakfast with a vacancy sign. The building was set back from the road and surrounded by a high wall covered in climbing roses, tucked well away from the main road through the small village. The vacancy sign near the gate swung on the breeze and was the only thing moving on the street. Mallory smiled and turned off the car. It was perfect. She stepped out of the car to the mingled scent of salt, ocean and roses.

She knocked tentatively on the door, and smiled the nervous smile of an inexperienced tourist when it swung open to reveal a woman with steel-grey hair and dark, piercing eyes.

'Hello.' She pointed at the vacancy sign. 'Do you have a single room available?'

The woman stared her up and down, her eyes resting for a moment on her backpack at her feet. 'You a tourist, lass, or an incomer from down south?'

Mallory hunched her shoulders nervously. 'Tourist. I haven't been in Scotland for long, and I need a place to stay.' She glanced over her shoulder toward the street. 'I don't know the area at all.'

The older woman's face softened. 'What's your name, then?'

Mallory flashed a quick, shy smile. 'Sarah Preston.'

'Well now, Sarah Preston, come inside and have a cup of tea.' The woman stepped to one side and gestured toward the dark hallway leading into the house.

Mallory rubbed her feet back and forth on the rough mat at the threshold before stepping through the door. She enjoyed the rough scratch of the fibre on the soles of her boots. It took her back to her childhood, to days of playing solo and cleaning boots so she could come inside for hot chocolate in front of the fire. A flash of another memory collided with the rest – her father yelling about wet tracks across the hall timbers, doors slamming, glasses breaking. She pulled back and tried to return to the earlier good feelings, which kept her going for longer than was necessary.

The other woman watched her, a small smile playing across her lips, as if she understood her quest for the nostalgias of childhood. When Mallory finally finished, the woman nodded her approval, walking ahead of her into the gloom of the house as she spoke.

'This way to the kitchen.' She pointed toward the end of the hallway.

Mallory caught a whiff of something dank, a drift of an earthy, slightly rotten odour in the air. She noticed the shadow of damp stains on the floor and lower walls of the hallway, and wrinkled her nose as she stepped over the darkened boards. A murmur of voices drifted through the damp walls into the warm silence of the hallway. The words hummed for a moment, then disappeared into the delicate notes of a piano concerto.

The older woman smiled. 'My eccentric neighbour in the next terrace, hen. He talks to himself, but he does play beautiful music.' She pushed the door at the end of the hallway open, and a wave of dry heat, saturated with the smell of fresh bread and coffee, enveloped Mallory.

The woman turned and smiled at her. 'I'm Agnes.' She gestured to a large wooden table. 'Take a seat, lass, I'm thinking you'll be hungry.'

She walked to the stove and lifted the lid on a pot, stirring the contents and sniffing her approval. The smell of bread and coffee gave way to the deeper, richer aroma of stew. The smell and the warmth reminded Mallory of her mother's kitchen. The rich scent of lamb, nutmeg and cloves wafted across the room, and her mouth started to water. She realised she was very hungry.

Agnes placed a cup of tea in front of her. 'What's that accent, then?'

Mallory took a mouthful of tea to hide her hesitation. 'North American – Arkansas.'

The older woman stared at Mallory, the challenge in her eyes unmistakeable. 'You dinnae sound American.'

Mallory placed her cup on the table and nodded. 'I've moved around a lot. I've been in New Zealand for six years. I'm taking the long way home.'

Agnes smiled. 'Aye, that's the spirit. Get out and see the world while you can. And what brings you to Plockton?'

Mallory grinned. 'I was told I shouldn't miss your Ceilidh.'

Agnes grinned back. 'Aye, that's true and all. You'll not find another dance to compare.' She stood and motioned toward the door. 'Come now, I'll show you your room.'

Mallory followed, elated that her interview had been successful. She wanted time to explore the village, find out about the locals. She wanted time to prepare.

When Agnes opened the door and ushered her into the room, Mallory had to suppress a grin at the huge four-poster bed with a tartan spread. It was exactly what she had hoped to find in a Scottish bed and breakfast. The room was homely and warm, with matching tartan curtains framing the view over the street.

Before she closed the door, Agnes looked at Mallory's backpack and asked, 'Do you have a dress for the Ceilidh, lass?'

'No.' Mallory kept her tone neutral to hide the rush of

frustration she felt at her own lack of planning. 'Is there a dress shop in town?'

Agnes laughed. 'Too late for that just now, and I'm doubting you'd be finding anything to your taste here, and all.' Her brow furrowed. 'But you cannae go to the dance in jeans, lass.' She looked Mallory up and down with a measuring eye. 'If you're of a mind, you can borrow a wee dress from my daughter's wardrobe. Heather would be the same size. She's away just now in Edinburgh, at the university.' She paused for a moment, staring pointedly at Mallory.

'How lovely. You must be so proud,' Mallory responded.

Agnes nodded, the glow of pride on her face deepening. 'Aye, that I am, lass, that I am. When you settle, come find me in the kitchen. We'll make you the belle of the ball.'

After Agnes closed the door, Mallory walked to the window and stared at the view. A pale, silver-blue light glowed over the village. She glanced along the road outside the bed and breakfast. The view was clear, unimpeded. The village sat silent and motionless beneath the silver-blue sky, as if it were suspended forever in a single moment of time. Her mind slipped back to another place, so different to this, where time had also seemed to stand still. She stared at the horizon, so close and filled with fluffy white clouds, so different to the endless horizon in Australia that still invaded her thoughts at every turn. She felt a stab of pain at the memory of Sam grinning as he watched kangaroos bounding toward the blue expanse above the gorge. She shook her head, pressing her fists into her eyes as she moved away from the window and dumped her backpack on the bed, focusing instead on the dance she would attend tonight. She couldn't keep torturing herself with thoughts of Sam, but when it came to her father, there was still hope. There was a chance the dance would be a dead end, yet there was also a chance that she would find out something that would take her a step closer to finding him. Besides, going to the Ceilidh had to be a better choice than hanging around in her room chewing on her memories, and she'd never experienced a traditional Scottish Ceilidh. Her curiosity was piqued.

~

The chiffon skirt of the layered dress floated around her legs in a soft cloud as Mallory walked toward the door of the Plockton Inn. She pulled the heavy overcoat closer, surprised to feel nervous butterflies fluttering and swooping in her stomach, and paused to smooth the emerald-green material of the skirt. Lively music floated out into the cool night air, led by the distinct notes of a fiddle. The merry lilt and fall of the music was irresistible, causing the stress of the past few weeks and the grief of losing Sam to lift for a moment. She stopped to watch the crowd silhouetted against the yellow glow of the window as they laughed and whirled in time with the music inside the inn. The feeling of familiarity she'd experienced at Applecross returned, and she stepped back into the darkness to stare up at the stars winking in the clear night above the inn, her chest contracting at the sense of homecoming she felt.

A wave of confusion and deep, gnawing sadness, surprising in its intensity, gripped her. Broken images flashed into her mind: sitting on her father's knee at a rough wooden table in front of an inn like this one, staring at the sparkling waters of a lake across a narrow road. The memory was not familiar – had she dreamed it? The world tilted for a moment and she leant forward, placing a shaking hand on the rough stone wall near the wooden door. She shook her head, taking deep breaths to steady herself, and decided it was time to make a move. She smoothed the skirt of the dress one last time and stepped through the door with Agnes' advice in mind. The older woman had been very firm about the rules of Ceilidh. Dance with everyone, enjoy yourself and expect the dance to get wildly physical. Mallory hesitated at the shouts of laughter and clinking of glass sounding over the music. The atmosphere inside the Plockton Inn was charged with the aromas of beer, cigarettes and whiskey, and felt thick and almost aggressive after the fresh openness of the night outside.

Mallory removed the heavy overcoat and hung it on an overloaded stand near the door. A young woman approached as she turned back to the bar, grinning as she grabbed Mallory by the hand. The woman swung her into the crowd, letting her go to be caught in the throng on the dancefloor. Mallory threaded from one person to the next, concentrating on keeping her feet under her as the tempo increased. After the fifth round through the crowd, she decided Agnes' choice of dress wasn't so bad after all. It had seemed too lightweight and summery for the weather, but it was perfect in the heated interior of the inn. After the sixth round, thirst got the better of her and she ducked under the arms of a waiting partner, breaking away from the dance to head toward the bar. There were already a few familiar faces along the bar, men and women who had passed her in the dance, their faces sweaty and wreathed with smiles. She leant against the bar and studied the whiskeys lining the opposite wall. Whiskey wasn't her favourite drink, but Agnes had been adamant that she must drink at least one.

The bartender stopped in front of her, one eyebrow raised. 'What will it be, lass?'

Mallory spotted a name that she remembered from her research into the area. 'I'll try a Torabhaig please.'

The bartender nodded his approval. 'You've chosen a good drop, then. How would you be knowing about our lovely Skye malt?'

She smiled as he placed a glass in front of her and poured the amber liquid straight from the bottle. 'My dad always loved whiskey, so I did some research before I left New Zealand. I wanted to try local distilleries.'

She turned away from the bar, watching the lively crowd while she sipped the drink. The heat hit her stomach and started to climb back up, finally flushing her cheeks. The alcoholic kick hit her at the same time, and she swirled the liquid slowly in the tumbler, studying the patterns it made on the glass. This would be her only alcoholic drink. She would have to drink water or pay the price tomorrow. She scanned the people scattered around the edges of the dance floor. There were a couple of redheads and the odd blonde, but the locals did not look like the typical Scots caricature seen in the childhood cartoons she'd loved so much. Most people here were small and wiry with pale skin, dark eyes and black hair. The music stopped and the crowd broke apart, with the bulk of the dancers streaming toward the bar. Mallory moved to one side, grinning at the good-natured jostling and laughter.

A tiny woman with jet black hair, blue eyes and ivory

skin turned to face her, thrusting out a hand while she waited for her drink. 'Hello, I'm Siobhan.'

Mallory shook her hand and leant in closer as the woman continued to speak rapidly in a heavy accent. 'You're not from around here, lass, but you would almost pass for a Cameron.' She turned to a young man standing beside her. 'Don't you think she looks like a Cameron, Johnny boy?'

The young man stared at Mallory with sudden hostility flashing in his eyes, but it was gone as quickly as it had occurred. 'C'mon Ma, ya cannae be wishing Cameron blood on anyone.'

His mother elbowed him, making him wince. 'Away there with your tongue, lad. There are ones who have died for saying less.' She scanned the bar. 'Don't forget walls have ears. Mind your opinions stay where they should.'

She tapped the side of her nose and turned back to Mallory. 'There's no need to be lonely at a Ceilidh, lass. Come sit with us.'

Mallory followed the pair to a corner table laden with empty glasses and surrounded by people shouting and laughing at each other. She slid onto a padded bench and tried to keep up as Siobhan reeled off introductions.

Johnny sat down beside her and raised his glass in a half salute. 'Let's toast our newest Ceilidh convert.'

Everyone at the table raised their glasses and cheered.

Johnny leaned close and winked. 'Me Ma's dreaming. You're ever too bonnie to be a Cameron.'

She blushed, raised her glass, and joined the toast to avoid answering.

The night passed in a blur of greetings, dancing, and wild promises to take her hunting in the Highlands, mountain climbing, and loch fishing. After the band packed up, Mallory slipped away from the thinning crowd, looking for a quiet place in the inn to rest. It had been an entertaining night, but nothing she had heard was useful or shed any light on the possible whereabouts of her father. She found a nook behind the back of the bar and sank into a pile of soft cushions. She wondered if everyone else's feet were aching as much as hers. The nook was pleasantly warm and the buzz of low conversation from the other booths was soothing. She leant back and surveyed the room, happy to keep off her feet until a large noticeboard on the opposite wall caught her attention. She stood up and walked to the board, reading about the history of Plockton and the surrounding areas with interest. It listed families that had been in the district for hundreds of years and the major events that had helped shape the community. The Cameron name caught her eye, and Johnny's comments came back to her. Unlike the other families listed, there was very little information, and no mention of any links to other Highland families in the area. She started to lose interest when a small photo in the bottom left corner of the board caught her eye. The caption read, *Cameron brothers win Loch Alsh Competition for third consecutive year.*

Mallory squatted down to get a better look, squinting at the grainy photo. The brothers were grinning at the camera, their fishing rods held high like trophies. They were both wiry in build and looked to be in their early teens. She moved closer to the image and decided John's estimation of the Cameron family wasn't entirely fair. The brothers were very different in appearance, but both were quite handsome in their own way. One was dark-haired with angular features and black eyes, the other was square-jawed with wavy, golden-red hair and an open, wide smile. Mallory's eyes widened and she felt her pulse quicken. The boys in the photo held very little resemblance to the men they had become, but there was no doubt in her mind who they were. A light sweat broke out on her forehead and she jumped up so quickly she felt faint. She leant on the wall for a moment, closing her eyes against the sudden spin of the room. She knew it was not caused by the single whiskey she had consumed hours ago, or the endless rounds of dancing. The photo was impossible, but there was no doubting what her eyes could see. The proof was there, right in front of her. Jimmy the Cat and her father were the Cameron brothers.

A hand touched her shoulder and she jumped.

'Steady, lass. I meant no harm,' said Johnny.

She smiled. 'It's okay. I'm tired, and I thought I was the only person back here now.'

He nodded at the noticeboard. 'I see you've spotted the infamous Cameron boys. Aye, they don't look like much, but there's not a man alive in the Highlands would cross them.'

'Do they still live here?'

He glanced at her, his expression unreadable. 'Who knows? They haven't been seen for over twenty years, but then, there's not a body around here that would go looking for them, you ken?'

She shook her head, careful to keep her expression neutral.

He looked over his shoulder, his body tense. 'They're supposed to be dead, but none will go near the Cameron bothy to check, lass. Highlanders dinnae go looking for trouble.'

She frowned. 'Do you mean to say nobody has been near their home for over twenty years?'

'Aye, that's exactly what I mean.'

He looked at the photo, his face pensive. 'They don't look much, but if they still live, they be a dangerous proposition. They have no friends in these parts. It were decided by all that it were best to leave the bothy well alone.'

'What about the authorities? They've never looked for them?'

He laughed. 'The Polis? They have better things to do than worry about the likes of the Cameron brothers.' He shrugged. 'Anyway, the Cameron family kept to their own and their land is tucked away on its own, too. I doubt the Polis even know where it is… a body would be unlucky to stumble across it.'

He paused and thrust out a hand. 'I wanted to say well met, lass, and safe travels. We're away home just now. We hope you enjoyed your first Ceilidh.'

After Johnny departed, Mallory turned back to the noticeboard with renewed interest. Sure, the Cameron land might be hard to find, but not impossible. She left the Plockton Inn, hunching into her overcoat against the chill air as she made her way back to the bed and breakfast.

Later that night, Mallory lay in her bed, turning the situation over in her mind. After the information she had received in Edinburgh, and the revelation at the Ceilidh, she felt certain her father would be living at the Cameron bothy. The main problem she could see now was finding it, because it was clear the locals would not help her, and asking too many questions would bring unwanted attention her way. She sat up and grabbed her laptop off the bedside table, tapped the search bar and brought up the Scottish Land Registry, but soon realised that searching for land owned by a family with a name like Cameron would be a slow and tedious exercise. She needed to narrow down the search.

She brought up a map of Scotland and focused on the area between Applecross and Plockton, triangulating out to the Isle of Skye. If the informant had been right, her father was somewhere between the mountains on the mainland and the Isle of Skye, but probably closer to Applecross than Plockton. She went back into the registry and narrowed her search to the area. There were four possible properties left, but two of them were too close to the coast. She narrowed in on the other two. One was beside a small Highland road, but the other appeared to be in an area so remote there was no road leading to it. She wrote down the information and hoped she could cross-reference it to a map and find enough information to get within a ten-kilometre radius of the property.

She lay back and stared out the window at the stars hanging in the midnight skies above Plockton. Somewhere out there, her father could once again be looking up at the same night sky, admiring the same stars. A shiver of anticipation ran through her. He was so close now. She could feel it.

~

The next morning, Mallory packed her bags, ready to sneak away before six, but the smell of bacon and coffee drew her to the kitchen.

Agnes looked up when she entered the room, her

eyebrows lifting. 'I thought you'd sleep in, lass. Ceilidh takes it out of a person.'

Mallory shrugged. 'I'm thinking about the coast, but I do want to see the Highlands. I was reading about some really beautiful wild areas yesterday.'

Agnes smiled as she placed a plate and coffee in front of her. 'What areas are those? It's best to plan, and the weather can change quite quickly. You dinnae want to find yourself lost up there, lass.'

She shrugged as she picked up her cutlery, and casually mentioned a valley near the isolated Cameron property she'd pinpointed the night before.

The woman stepped back from the table as though she had been burnt. 'Now, why would you be wanting to go there?' she cried.

Mallory felt her stomach clench at the panic in the older woman's voice. 'I thought it looked wild and untouched. I thought I would see some wildlife there, for sure. Is it a bad idea?' she asked, keeping her expression mild and slightly bored.

'Yes!' Agnes sat down beside her, placing a hand on hers. 'Lass, there are plenty of beautiful places to photograph wildlife in Scotland. That area is not one of them.' She stood up, her expression suddenly guarded. 'It's been said that a lot of tourists have gone missing up that way. You'd be better sticking to the coast, or perhaps driving to Isle of Skye.'

The woman's reaction strengthened Mallory's resolve. She knew she was on the right track. She lifted her coffee cup to her mouth to hide her reaction, widened her eyes and said, 'I don't want to get lost in the Highlands, Agnes. I like my comfort too much.' She took another sip of her coffee and took the paper map out of her bag. 'I need some natural wildlife shots, or I won't get paid. Can you recommend somewhere along the coast that isn't overrun with tourists?'

The older woman exhaled with obvious relief. 'Now there then, that's a better idea, lass.' She sat down beside Mallory, smoothing the map with her hands, and traced the West Coast with her index finger, pinpointing places of beauty and interest that were not usual tourist destinations.

She marked the places Agnes pointed out with a pen and wrote a rough itinerary in her notebook to ensure that the older woman was convinced she would travel to the coast.

After breakfast, Mallory packed her bags into her car and drove toward the main road through the village. She looked in the mirror, saw Agnes watching her vehicle, and flicked her indicator in the direction of the coast. She glanced at the map and smiled. If anyone asked, the woman would say Mallory was intending to tour the coastline. She drove along the main road through the village, slowing to wave at the group of men who had observed her arrival yesterday. They tipped their hats as she passed. She smiled as she drove to the next intersecting road outside of the village and turned back, skirting around Plockton toward her true destination in the mountains.

~

Sam reached Plockton and grinned at a group of old men watching his car rolling along the street toward the Plockton Inn. He knew there would be no chance for a stranger to avoid attention in this village. There were five men and two women sitting at the bar when he entered, and they all turned to stare, their conversation suspended in favour of observing his entrance. He gave a friendly nod as he approached and ordered a half-pint of Tennent's. He leant against the bar and waited. It was never a good strategy to lead with questions in tight-knit communities. It would only be a matter of time until curiosity got the better of one of the patrons, and they asked the questions instead. He sipped his beer and watched the man to the right of him out of the corner of his eye. He looked ancient, with bushy grey eyebrows, wild hair and heavily wrinkled skin.

He glanced at Sam every so often, with a deep frown forming between his brows. 'Hallo there, you're not from these parts. Where's your home, then?'

Sam nodded. 'Australia.'

The old man stared at him, the challenge in his gaze palpable.

Sam smiled. 'I'm on holidays. I was supposed to meet a distant cousin here yesterday, but I got held up.'

The man half nodded and took a slow draught of his beer. 'Bad luck or bad management?'

'Bad management on my part, and bad luck with a storm near Applecross.'

'At least you're an honest one, lad.' The man turned to the other patrons in the bar. 'Have there been any incomers through town in the last few days?'

The four chorused, 'Aye, the wee lassie at the Ceilidh.'

One of the men lifted his glass in a casual salute. 'Well met. Would that be the cousin you were expecting to meet? The bonnie lass from New Zealand?'

Sam nodded. 'Do you know if she's still here?'

The man shrugged. 'Cannae say. She was staying at the

bed and breakfast. You could try there. Next right-turn off the main road, less than half a mile up the street.'

Sam raised his glass in return. 'Thank you, fellas, much appreciated.'

Once he was back in his car, Sam let out a low whoop of excitement. He was getting close, might be even closer than he thought. His mind tried to wander back into memory, but he refused to let his thoughts stray and kept his focus on the current situation. Whatever he and Mallory had in the past was gone. There was only the present.

He swung onto the main street and took the next right, idling past neat cottages and seaside terraces until he found the bed and breakfast. He sat in front of the terrace house, watching the vacancy sign swinging in the breeze. What if she were in there now, having breakfast? He scanned the area, looking for a red Renault, but there were very few vehicles parked on the road, and none of them were that make. As he stepped out of the car, he knew it was very likely she was already on the move.

A woman opened the door after his first knock and stared him up and down. 'I saw you looking at my sign. Are you wanting a room, lad?'

He shook his head. 'No, thank you. I was just at the pub. I was told my cousin may have stayed here.'

The woman folded her arms. 'Cousin?'

Sam saw the open distrust in her eyes. He smiled and stepped back a little before leaning on the handrail. 'Yeah. I was supposed to meet her last night, but...' He spread his hands with palms upraised to indicate circumstances beyond his control.

The woman watched him without smiling. A twitch

developed on one temple and her eyes darkened slightly. 'A lass you say?' She raised an eyebrow when he nodded. 'Well, she's not here now, lad. She's long gone.' She raised a hand to her chin, her fingers partially covering her mouth as she spoke. 'She said something about heading back toward the East Coast today.'

Sam nodded and said his thanks before she shut the door in his face. The woman was lying, but that wasn't much help to him. The only thing he could be sure of now was that Mallory wasn't heading back toward the East Coast.

He decided to go back to the inn. He took a map and guidebook he'd bought in Edinburgh into the inn and found a quiet nook away from the bar. He slid into the booth, spread the map across the table, and started cross-referencing places of note with the map. An hour later, he sat back, frustrated. He had no doubt Mallory was on the West Coast for a good reason, but nothing presented itself as a likely lead. He pressed two fingers into his eyes to relieve the ache and looked around the snug bar until a large board caught his eye. He decided to stretch his legs and take a look at the board. He walked over, running his eye over the usual history of buildings and families until a photo of two brothers holding fishing rods caught his eye. He leant in a little closer to read the caption below the photo. He stared at the photo again, not quite believing what his eyes were seeing. He walked back out to the bar and ordered a toasted sandwich. The group of men and women had dispersed, and only the old timer who had spoken to him earlier remained.

The man turned to him, eager to share information. 'Well now, I've spoken to our watchers on the street. They said the bonnie lassie in the red car was heading toward the coast.'

Sam nodded his thanks, his expression neutral. 'I'll keep an eye out for her.' He slid onto a barstool beside the man, and said, 'I read the history on the board back there. What's a bothy?'

'It's a wee cottage. Some folk live in them all year round and some folk use them as refuge when they're hiking. There's few will refuse you shelter in the Highlands.' He took a draught of his beer, his face pensive. 'Aye, but they're often basic. No electricity and the like.'

Sam nodded. 'I'm thinking of heading into the mountains. I saw some families mentioned on the board – like the Camerons and the MacDonalds. Do Highland families still live in the mountains?'

The old man's face paled. When he spoke, his voice was barely a whisper. 'We don't say *that* name here, lad.' He placed his beer on the bar with a shaking hand. 'You'll not be wanting to go near Cameron land, lad – they are the few who would do you harm, now. There's not a soul here knows if they're alive or dead, and that's how we'll be wanting to keep it, aye.' He crossed himself and looked skyward. 'Anyway, their land is a long way from civilisation, thanks be to the Gods.' He offered a weak smile. 'On the other hand, if you're of a mind to see the Highlands, you'll find the MacDonalds quite hospitable. They'll not begrudge you using a bothy.'

The barman arrived with Sam's food. He said his thanks and went back to the nook. While he ate, he traced a road into the Highlands with his finger, following the few smaller roads that branched off into apparent wilderness, and wondered which one led to the Cameron bothy and Warwick Cash.

~

The road narrowed and the forest became denser, crowding in closer to the vehicle as Mallory travelled further into the Highlands. She pulled to a halt, turned the radio off and wound down the window. A freezing breeze ushered in a deep silence, punctuated by birdsong and the occasional huff of wind through trees. The scent of pine, followed by the subtle undertones of moss, fungi and a woody fragrance that could have been heather or forest, filled the car. She smiled as a vague memory flashed, of sinking into deep winter snow as she ran through rows of pines in her pink wellington boots and yellow raincoat. Another memory surfaced, of rolling snowballs with her father and throwing them at her brother. It was clearer than the first and filled her with a nostalgia that was quickly replaced by confusion. She searched for context on the memories, feeling sure they must relate to her childhood in Canada, but they seemed firmly anchored in the landscape surrounding her. They seemed part of the Scottish Highlands.

She stared at the forest marching up out of the glens on either side of the road and felt her confusion deepen. This country was familiar, but she had no recollection of living in Scotland, especially after discovering the photo of her father at Plockton. She shrugged and opened her map against the steering wheel. No doubt her father could answer these questions, so it was best to keep moving and concentrate on finding him. She followed the faint line of the road she'd traversed and realised it would finish approximately ten kilometres before she reached her target.

Mallory stared at the tiny track winding ahead. The way it disappeared into the darkening forest caused a slight twinge of apprehension. She glanced at her watch. She had to keep going. She still had five hours of daylight and wanted to reach the Cameron bothy before dark. She started the car and considered the roar of the engine in the silence of the glens. If she wanted an element of surprise, she would have to ditch the car and walk the last leg of her return to her father.

Mallory surveyed the area. Nothing moved and there was no sign of human habitation. She'd be unlucky if anyone found her car up here. She idled toward a small clearing on the side of the road and parked the car behind a stand of trees that partially shielded it from the road. She hiked at full pace until she saw a barely visible track off to one side that led upwards onto a wild, seemingly untouched mountain. She slung her backpack off her shoulders, consulted the map and then started along the path. As she walked, the dappled late afternoon light fell on mosses and mushrooms on the forest floor, and Mallory lifted her face to the soft mist of clouds that were beginning to descend onto the path. She suspected darkness would fall quickly and increased her pace. The path became fainter, until it was almost impossible to follow.

Mallory hesitated and was about to check her bearings when she spotted a pinpoint of light through a dense, overgrown hedge on her left. She skirted along the foliage until she managed to push through a small gap in the branches, popping out into a clearing. The openness was completely unexpected after the density of the forest, and it revealed a substantial stone bothy on the rise above her, with a roof covered in darkened thatch and walls stained from years of weather. The setting of the building was breathtaking, with a stand of trees curled around one side of the building and stairs that had been cut into the slope of the land leading to a small loch in front of the bothy. Beyond the immediate surrounds was an endless view of mountains, valleys and lochs. Mallory's pulse leapt and she had to suppress the urge to let out a whoop. She knew this had to be the Cameron bothy, and the light told her someone was in residence. She popped back through the gap, skirting the hedge until she was across from the stand of trees, where she dropped on all fours to crawl to the other side. Once there, she moved silently through the trees until she was level with a window.

The light inside illuminated an orderly room with rows of books and artworks along the walls. A woman with black hair sat near a bay window opposite, her gaze turned outward to the view beyond. Someone shifted in a chair closer to the window, a flash of grey hair appearing over the back before disappearing. Mallory crouched and watched the scene for fifteen minutes, but no other people appeared and the couple in the room seemed unarmed and relaxed. She waited another five minutes, then decided there was no point crouching outside the bothy all night. She made her way to the door above the stairs to the loch and knocked. A deep voice, laced with aggressive suspicion, sounded from within, followed by a placatory feminine reply. Footsteps approached and she stepped to one side of the doorway, using the jamb as cover. She realised she was holding her breath as the door swung open. The outline of a man holding a shotgun, backlit by the hall, appeared in the doorway.

She exhaled, raised her hands above her head with open palms faced toward the doorway, and said, 'Hello, Father.'

8

THE man in the doorway grunted in surprise at the sound of Mallory's voice. He dropped the shotgun to his side. 'Mally? What the hell are you doing here?'

'Do you mean, how did I find you?' Mallory started to lower her arms and saw the shotgun lift at her father's side. She slowed her movements, keeping her arms away from her body and her palms visible.

Warwick looked beyond his daughter, scanning the tree line for any sign of movement. The barrel of the gun dropped toward the floor again. 'If anyone could find me, it would be you, my darling lass.'

The deep timbre of his voice hit her in the chest, and the turmoil of emotion it caused constricted her throat. The Scottish lilt was new, but the voice was the same one that sang her lullabies when she was a small child. She waited, not wanting her emotions to explode all over her father in the first five minutes of meeting. He stepped back a little, bringing his face into the light in the hallway. Momentary shock gripped Mallory. He seemed shorter, and she wasn't expecting the wrinkles and the greying beard.

He smiled. 'We're all growing older, lass.'

She caught a hint of pain in his voice. He had always caught the attention of women in the past; he had been so proud of his appearance. She imagined that ageing probably bothered him. A woman with lustrous ivory skin, dark eyes and dark hair appeared at the other end of the hall and glided toward them. Mallory felt a small stab of satisfaction at her previous deduction.

The woman stopped just short of the doorway. 'Warwick? Who is our visitor?'

Mallory detected a savage undertone of jealousy and suppressed the urge to smirk. Clearly, some things never changed.

He stepped sideways, keeping both Mallory and the woman in his line of view. 'Iona, this is my daughter, Mally.'

Mallory waited for an explanation of Iona's presence, but the three stood awkwardly, the silence of the night pushing around them like a living thing.

Iona stepped forward with a smile and outstretched hand. 'Come in, lassie. It's getting cold out.'

Warwick inclined his head and Mallory knew in that instant that he didn't want her in the bothy. She covered her hurt with a megawatt smile as she took Iona's hand and stepped over the threshold. Her father moved to one side, his reluctance to invite her inside still obvious. She pushed the hurt down further and focused on the reason she had come. Finally, she had a chance to get her questions answered.

He waited until she stepped past him before following both women along the hallway into the main room of the bothy. Mallory could feel him measuring her, assessing the risk she posed to him. She turned to face him when they reached the main room and noticed he still carried the shotgun.

He followed her gaze and shrugged. 'You've made it this far. You know a person can't be too careful.' He motioned toward a chair near the bay window. 'Take a seat, lass. Iona will make you a cup of tea.'

The other woman disappeared into a small room off the main room.

Mallory took in the fine art on the rough-hewn wooden walls, the sculptures taking pride of place in the bay window and the silk-covered cushions on the leather chesterfield. 'You still like the finer things in life.'

Warwick frowned. 'And why not?'

'A family with barely enough means to get through winter.' She glared at him, and he looked toward the loch outside the window.

'You wouldn't understand.' His voice was distant, his expression taut with anger.

'Try me.'

His face reddened as he swung toward her and raised the shotgun. He opened his mouth, but his next words were drowned by hammering on the same door that Mallory had entered.

His face went a darker shade of red. 'Did you bring someone with you?'

She shook her head. 'No way.' She stood up, keeping her arms loose at her sides. 'But I guess that's the problem, isn't it, old man? If I found you, others can.'

His face went a darker shade of red. 'You most likely led others here.'

Mallory shook her head. 'You taught me well. If others have found you, it's on you. It has nothing to do with me.'

The hammering started again and he motioned to her to be quiet. He moved toward the door, his back pressed to the wall of the hallway, the sawn-off raised and ready.

'Mr C, it's me, William. I need to speak to you… It's, well, it's urgent.'

Warwick's body relaxed and he dropped the barrel of the gun toward the floor as he flung the door open. 'What the hell are you doing coming to the bothy, lad?'

Mallory caught a glimpse of a young, slightly-built man before he stepped back out of the light in the doorway.

Warwick closed the door behind him. She could hear the murmur of their voices, heard the words 'stranger' and 'safe place'. She was about to move toward the door when it reopened and Warwick appeared alone.

He stared at her without speaking for what seemed like an eternity.

When he did speak, she felt the latent anger beneath his words. 'There's been an Australian fellow poking around Plockton.' He paused, rubbing his thumb along the stock of the shotgun. 'Would you know anything about that?'

Mallory nodded. 'I'm sure you already know about the Australian lawman. Is it him?'

Warwick frowned, as if her admission disappointed him. 'Yes, lass. Everyone knows. He's followed you here.' He snorted, his disgust apparent. 'Seems I didn't teach you near well enough, then.' He lifted his free hand and rubbed his forehead. 'We can neutralise the situation.'

Fear for Sam's safety coiled in Mallory's stomach. She kept her voice steady and asked, 'What do you intend to do?'

Warwick grinned, his expression cold. 'He's outside, lass. Apparently, he has intel about Trafford.' His grin dropped. 'He knows how to get a live foot in the door, I'll give him that much. But rest assured, if he's lying, he won't be leaving boots first.'

He walked back to the door, swinging it open to reveal the young man and Sam on the step. Mallory felt her stomach lurch at the sight of him. Her heart started to pound and she wondered if she would make a fool of herself and faint. She shook her head. No, she wasn't about to make a fool out of herself over a lawman. She was made of stronger stuff. When he stepped into the hallway, she took in his gaunt face and the crumpled state of his clothes. He had obviously been put through it trying to find her. She felt a stab of anger. If he were smart, he would forget about her and the Topaz Stallion and go back to Australia.

Sam looked at her and nodded.

Warwick watched them both and laughed. 'What have we here, then? A romantic Highland reunion? I'd like to say congratulations, but you have less than five minutes, lad. Dinnae be wasting it on niceties.'

'Trafford is on his way. I saw one of his goons at a village on the coast. They have no reason to be in Scotland, except for you, Warwick.' He glanced at Mallory, 'Oh, and you too, of course.'

Mallory's lip twitched into a half snarl. He didn't need to sound so smug.

'Well to be sure, they could be anywhere up here. Probably not even close.'

'That's the problem. I saw the same guy at the local pub in Achmore. That's only forty-five minutes away.'

Warwick's eyes narrowed. He shut the door and turned to his daughter. 'Mally, we're taking your boyfriend for a drive.'

Mallory shook her head and stepped backwards. 'He's not my boyfriend. Leave him out of it.'

Warwick smiled, his eyes cold. 'Too late. He's here and he's involved.' He nodded toward the closed door. 'Understand now, he can't stay here. I hold you responsible. I'm taking him away from the bothy. With or without you.'

Mallory's legs felt heavy as she followed her father toward the door. He stepped onto the porch and told Sam a lame joke about Australia. The two men laughed and chatted about the weather as they walked toward the vehicle at the side of the building. The entire scene seemed surreal, almost cartoonish. She wanted to turn around and walk away, but there was nowhere to go and she didn't trust her father to keep Sam safe.

Warwick unlocked the vehicle and nodded at the pair to get in. He walked toward a shed near the house and disappeared inside.

Mallory climbed into the front seat of the Range Rover, acutely aware of Sam sitting behind her.

He leant forward and she felt the weight of his arm resting on her seat. 'You know I have to take you and your father in, Mallory.'

Warwick walked out of the shed with a duffel bag slung over his shoulder and a spurt of fear shot through Mallory. 'You'll be lucky to leave Scotland alive. You should forget about all of this and go home.' She turned slightly and looked into his eyes. 'I don't trust my father.'

Sam squeezed her shoulder. 'I figured you'd see that.'

She shrugged him off. 'He's still my father, and you are a lawman. I don't understand what you hope to achieve.' She raised an eyebrow. 'Besides going home in a body bag.'

Warwick jumped into the driver's side, dropped the bag beside her feet and started to reverse at speed as he spoke. 'I have a hunting hide about ten miles north-west of here. No one knows it's there. We will be safe there while we work out a plan to neutralise Trafford and his people.'

'What about Iona?'

He looked at Mallory, his face earnest. 'She knows what to do. Don't worry about her. We have to get rid of Trafford. If he thinks he can get his hands on the Stallion, he'll not stop.'

Mallory hunched into the seat. 'I know. He's been after me for an opal and I don't have it.'

He stared at her, his expression unreadable, and then concentrated on manoeuvring the vehicle along the rutted driveway, his face crinkling into a pained wince every time branches screeched along the sides. When he reached the end of the track, his hands tightened on the wheel while he surveyed the empty road. He rubbed a finger across the ring on his pinkie as he glanced in the rear mirror. 'You know you won't be taking me or the Stallion anywhere, lad.'

Mallory glared at him. 'Can't you just give the stupid ring up, Dad? For everyone's sake?'

His hands tightened further. 'Do you think giving it to a lawman will stop Trafford, lass?' he asked, his voice loud in the silence of the cab.

He took a deep breath and loosened his grip on the wheel. 'We'll head to the hide. We won't be disturbed up there.' He nodded. 'We need to focus on a plan, just now.'

He glanced in the mirror again. 'We'll be safe up there.'

Sam nodded without answering. Mallory glanced over her shoulder at him, but it was hard to tell what he was thinking. She felt a stab of suspicion at her father's words. It made no sense to go to a deserted mountain to make plans, but at least the goons who had tracked Warwick to the village would have trouble finding him at an unknown hide, and there was no way any locals would help them onto Cameron land.

She wondered for a moment if her father had weapons at the hide. She felt the pressure of Sam's gaze and kept her eyes forward. She knew he had watched the interaction between her and her father, and no doubt already worked out that she didn't know him at all. Whatever Warwick was up to, she could admit to herself that she had no idea. Her father slowed the car and pulled into a deserted layby, creeping the vehicle along a narrowing path until it was completely screened behind a stand of trees. He pointed to a barely visible track leading toward a lower peak. 'We'll get going up there.'

Sam looked around. There was nothing but mountain heath, and a steep glen filled with thick pines below. He frowned. 'No one can see us here. Why not make plans in the car? Why do we need to walk up a mountain?'

Warwick glanced at him in the rear mirror. 'You'd be surprised who is watching in these parts. It's an extra precaution, son. In case anyone is about. We can get the jump, because we'll have a good head start up there.'

Sam glanced at Mallory, but she reefed the door open and slid out of the car before he could stop her, hopping from foot to foot to keep warm. He stepped out on the other side of the vehicle. A chill wind blew across the mountain, pushing misty clouds over the glen. He shivered and zipped his jacket over the layers of clothing beneath until it was firm around his neck.

He looked at Warwick, his lips pressed together in a suspicious line. 'I am not leaving Mallory on her own, and you know I'm not leaving without you and that ring in custody,' he said.

Warwick shook his head, a slight smile on his face. 'Now son, don't go making promises you can't keep. Better than you have tried and failed to get this ring.' His eyes went cold. 'If my daughter wasn't so besotted with you, and if you didn't have information that I may need, I would have dispatched you already.'

'Dad?' Mallory stared at her father in horror.

He changed tack, spreading his hands wide, his tone placating. 'Okay, you two, I really hope you'll listen to some sense. We need to get to the hide, get some supplies and split up, go our separate ways. You both need to get as far away from me as possible.' He rubbed his jaw contemplatively. 'As a matter of fact, it would be perfect if we could make it appear like you've both died up here.'

'Would you really kill someone?' Mallory interrupted.

Warwick looked at her as if he had forgotten she was there. 'I'm a criminal, Mally, and so are you. Don't pretend you wouldn't remove a person who threatened your freedom.'

She shook her head. 'No! I wouldn't kill anyone!'

His reached out and touched her arm, his expression almost pained. 'Then you are already a dead woman walking, my dear.' He slung the duffel over his shoulder and turned toward the track. 'Let's get to the hide for now. We can argue about the morality of survival of the fittest there.'

Sam hesitated. 'How do we know you're not leading us into a trap?'

'Come on now, I didn't even know you existed until you turned up at my door. Let's face it, I could have shot you there.' He stood for a moment as if contemplating the scenario he had just described, before continuing. 'So, you'll have to take my word – unless you have a better option?'

Warwick put an arm around Mallory's shoulders, herding her toward the track and away from Sam. He raised his voice and kicked through shale on the track as he spoke. 'It seems we are at an impasse. What would you suggest, Lawman?'

Mallory could feel Sam watching them and wondered what he intended to do. There was no mistaking the threat in her father's voice, but she felt certain he wouldn't attack Sam for no reason. She wondered if Sam was armed, and if he would shoot her father. She pushed the thought away immediately. She knew Sam wouldn't kill another human unless they posed an immediate threat, and if he killed her father, she would never forgive him. She heard him following them up the track, his footfall soft on the needles and moss beneath the stands of thinning trees until they reached an escarpment and started to pick their way between boulders and patchy heather. Heavy clouds drifted over the trio, dropping until they were barely visible to each other. Fog enveloped Mallory and Warwick, and she felt a frisson of danger when the soft footfalls behind them ceased. She pulled back from her father, stopping to probe the dense fog for movement when she heard the unmistakeable crunch of metal hitting bone.

Mallory heard the thud of a body hitting the ground and reefed her arm free from her father, running back along the path. She let out a scream at the sight of Sam on the path. She lunged toward his motionless body, gasping at the deep, bleeding gash on the side of his head.

Jimmy the Cat appeared out of the mist and winked at her. 'Well, well. We always seem to meet at the most inopportune moments, don't we, young Cash.'

Warwick reappeared beside her and Jimmy started to laugh.

He stared at Jimmy with wild eyes, grabbed Mallory's hand and yelled, 'Run!'

They ran up the narrow track toward the lower peak. Mallory was aware of the thud of their boots on the rocky path and the hoarse sounds of their breathing. She strained her ears but couldn't hear sounds of pursuit behind them. Her thoughts flew to Sam, and she slowed down, trying to pull her hand out her father's grip. Sam was on the ground, defenceless. Jimmy could be doing anything to him right now.

Warwick jerked on her arm and muttered, 'Don't worry about the lawman. Jimmy disabled him. He won't bother with him unless he wakes. Best you worry about yourself, girl. He'll slit both our throats without a minute's thought.'

He dragged her with him toward a dense thicket on the lower summit, then stopped and stared into the thick clouds behind them, before half-turning to whisper, 'It's easy to get lost up here. So many tracks and dead ends.'

Mallory was panting from the run, and gasped, 'Jimmy

is here for the Stallion, isn't he? Give him that stupid ring, Dad.'

Warwick flinched. 'Even if I did, it wouldn't make any difference to your safety, or mine. Listen to sense, girl.'

'I want to go back. Sam needs help.'

He shook his head. 'We can't help him now.' He glared at her. 'No point us all getting killed over a useless copper.'

Heavy clouds dropped, enveloping the pair.

'We're about to lose visibility, Dad. This isn't safe.'

Warwick's hand tightened on hers. 'I don't need to see where I'm going. I know these mountains inside out.'

'You seem to forget that I also know these mountains!' Jimmy's voice was impossible to locate in the fog.

Mallory froze and peered into the mist that swirled around them. She stared at her father, hoping he could create a miracle.

'Do you remember when we used to run through the glens here, Wally?' Jimmy's voice boomed in the deepening fog around them. 'Do you remember, lad, us pretending we were clansmen hunting the dirty English lords?'

Mallory frowned at Warwick. He lifted his finger to his lips.

'Aye,' said Jimmy. 'You weren't the mighty Warwick Cash then, you were my twin brother, War. The one person I thought I could always trust.'

Warwick glanced at Mallory. 'No surprises, lass? You knew?'

She nodded and he shrugged.

'But does she know about the heists we pulled? Does she know about the people we killed for sport?'

Mallory's eyes widened. She looked at her father, but he

would not meet her gaze. She twisted in his grip, applying force to a pressure point and locking his hand backwards until he released her hand.

'Wait, don't step away! You're not safe up here,' he cried as she moved out of his reach.

An arm snaked out of the fog behind her, curling around her neck like living rope. Jimmy lifted her in a quick, efficient movement, and held her in front of him like a shield.

'Behave and I'll give you your air,' he said.

She nodded and he dropped her onto her feet, releasing his grip by the smallest margin. Jimmy leant in so close she could feel the press of his chest on her back and his breath on her neck. She tried to recoil, but he held her firm.

'You double-crossed me,' he said to Warwick. 'I waited all those years in jail for a sign. Anything to let me know you hadn't shopped me for the Topaz Stallion.'

Warwick shook his head. 'Come on, wee Jimmy. You know I didn't shop you. It were an unfortunate circumstance. What point would there have been to handing myself in? We would have been in a bigger pickle if we were both locked up.'

Jimmy laughed. 'I never expected you to shop yourself to the Heat. I did expect to see you when I got out. I did expect to find out who could have shopped me, if not my twin brother.'

It was Warwick's turn to laugh. 'I know how your mind works. I was young. I didn't want to die.'

Jimmy's grip tightened around Mallory's neck. 'Give me the ring, or I will kill her.'

Warwick shook his head. 'No. We both know you'll kill

her anyway.'

Mallory saw the weapon in Jimmy's hand and tried to warn her father, but he tightened his strangling grip and fired the gun, grazing Warwick's wrist.

Warwick yelped and clutched his bleeding arm to his body as he rolled away into the murky clouds.

'Ring!' Jimmy barked and fired another shot into the fog. 'You owe me, big brother. It is my turn.'

Warwick reappeared, blood dripping from his wrist as he twisted the ring off his finger. He spat at Jimmy's boots, his face twisted with rage and hatred. 'You were always stupid! You won't have it for long, you hot-headed idiot.'

He walked as close to Jimmy and Mallory as he dared and placed the ring on the ground. Mallory watched him in disbelief. His actions made no sense. She knew he couldn't be threatened into releasing the Topaz Stallion. He had refused to give the ring up for her and was prepared to give up his life rather than parting with it, yet now he placed it with loving care on the ground in front of his brother because it was "his turn".

Jimmy gave a guttural snort at the sight of the ring. He tightened his grip on Mallory and twisted down, taking her with him as he picked up the ring. She let her body relax and went with him. There would be no hope of escape later if she were injured now.

~

Jimmy ran behind Mallory along the path, his iron fingers locked around her wrists.

She tried to slow down and he shoved her forward. 'Don't try to get loose, or I'll break both your wrists.'

Mallory relaxed into the pace so she wouldn't stumble

and fall. She let the muscles in her arms go loose and surveyed the terrain around them. The sight of Sam lying bleeding and motionless on the path behind them kept returning to her. Silent tears streamed down her face and the pain in her chest was unbearable. If he wasn't already dead, he would die of exposure on this mountain. Her mind recoiled from the thought. It was impossible to imagine a world without Sam in it. She wanted to collapse onto the ground and howl, but the pain of Jimmy twisting her wrists kept her focused on her current predicament. The clouds had cleared and she could see the mountain sloping upwards into a sea of purple heather to her right. There was no point trying to go uphill. The left side of the path was covered in jagged rocks and dropped away at some point below her vision. She lengthened her stride to better match the rhythm of Jimmy's and waited, knowing that she would have to take any opportunity that arose if she wanted to get out of the Highlands alive.

The sound of Warwick crashing through the heather as he bellowed Jimmy's name echoed around the glen.

Jimmy chuckled. 'I knew he'd come after me.' He jerked her arm. 'Did you notice your old man wouldn't give up the Stallion for you? He won't give it to Trafford to get you off the hook either.' He laughed, the sound low and nasty. 'And he won't let me keep it while he has breath in his body. Leopards never change their spots, young Cash.'

Mallory's gut clenched. 'Why did he give it to you?'

He laughed. 'That is our secret.'

'You've got the ring. What more do you want?' she asked.

Jimmy tapped her wrist with a light finger. 'I told you

I'd take it off his dead hand, but this is better.'

'He'll kill you,' Mallory panted.

Jimmy let out a bark of laughter. 'Not likely. War isn't coming to save you, little one. This is personal. He wants his Stallion back. He knows if he can take it off me now, we're square.' He shoved the small of her back. 'But that isn't going to happen, because I'll kill him first.' He jerked her arm again. 'Now, less chat!'

She stumbled, and he lifted her by her wrists. 'Keep your feet under you, girl!' Pain shot up her arms into her elbows and her shoulders burned. She forced her muscles to relax and stay with the rhythm.

They rounded a corner and jogged along a rougher, narrower section of the path. Jimmy stumbled on a rock and Mallory took what she knew may be her only chance to get away. She fell forward and rolled, ignoring her screaming shoulder joints as she used her bodyweight to throw him over the top of her toward the deep drop-off to her left. He grunted as he hit the ground, his grip loosening for a moment. She pulled one arm free and slid her fingers into the sheath strapped under her shirt. His grip tightened on her remaining hand as they tumbled over the rocks and down the slope. Shale started to rain down the hill with them. It dug into her skin, cutting and burning as she rolled with Jimmy. She hit a large boulder and flinched at the sudden flare of pain before her thigh went dead. Her eyes were streaming from the pain but she could see Jimmy's face close to hers, his teeth bared, his eyes black with empty rage. He reached toward her throat with his free hand as she drew the knife out of the sheath and plunged it between his ribs. His eyes widened in shock, and he let her go. Blood flowed past the hilt of the knife, staining the slope as they continued to slide, their eyes trained on each other.

Mallory hit a tree stump and stopped with a jerk strong enough to break Jimmy's grip. The wind was knocked out of her and she gasped for breath as she watched him continue to slide away. He snatched at a large rock on the edge of the escarpment and their eyes locked for a moment, and then he was gone, his scrabbling hands the last thing she saw before he disappeared over the side into the silent void below. She waited for what seemed an eternity before a dull thud rose from the floor of the valley. She closed her watering eyes for a moment, holding back tears that threatened to engulf her.

An avalanche of shale continued to slide down the slope, rolling over her like deadly hail as it fell off the side of the cliff. She opened her eyes and stared at the sky above her. It looked so peaceful and calm, and she started to drift until her dead leg came back to life and began to throb. She tried to move it and almost screamed with the pain. It didn't want to cooperate. There was no way she could get back up the slope, not with the shale sliding in the opposite direction. She increased her grip on the tree. She would not give up.

'Mallory!'

She turned her head at the sound of her father's voice, but she couldn't see him from her position.

'Down here,' she called out.

'Where's Jimmy?'

Mallory frowned. 'Does that matter right now? I'm kinda in a spot here, Dad.'

'Don't want to get jumped halfway down.'

'Don't worry. He went over the side.'

'Where's the Stallion?'

'Dad? Really?'

'Yes, of course.' Warwick's voice seemed further away.

'Where are you going?'

'I'm securing a rope. Hang in there.'

Mallory felt her body relax. She had suspected her father would leave her on the side of the mountain to pursue the ring, but he was proving her wrong. Perhaps Jimmy didn't know his brother as well as he thought he did?

She concentrated on the sound of Warwick's approach and tried to block out the anxiety caused by the constant sound of shale raining over the edge of the cliff. When he reached her, Warwick tied an extra length of the rope attached to his body around her.

'This isn't ideal, but it will have to do.'

'Where did the rope come from?'

He looked at her for a moment. 'I taught you better. One should always be prepared, lass.' She remembered his duffel bag and felt her skin prickle with embarrassment. She felt fourteen-years-old again in the face of his contempt.

They struggled up the slope, hand over hand along the rope as the last vestiges of afternoon light descended into chilly dusk.

When they reached the path, Mallory sunk onto a large boulder and felt her legs start to shake.

'I'm going to see if Jimmy is alive,' said Warwick.

'What about Sam?'

He put a soft hand on her shoulder. 'It's too late for him, girl.'

'We can't leave him here!'

Her father's face darkened. 'What are we supposed to do with him? He's gone, and we can't take him anywhere.'

'But, how can you know that. How can—'

'Stop!' Her father's voice echoed off the mountains, making her jump. 'I went back to the car for the rope, see. I checked on him, of course. He's gone.'

She shook her head and tried to push past him.

He grabbed her shoulders, holding her at arm's length. 'Think about it, Mallory. We can't take him to the authorities. What would we say?' He frowned. 'And imagine if a cop pulls us over and we've got a dead lawman in the car?' He gave her a gentle shake. 'Besides, you don't want to see him now, you don't want to remember him like that.' He pulled her into his arms. 'I did the best I could, lass. I moved him. He's under a thicket of heather where he can rest in peace.' He lifted her chin and wiped her tears. 'Now pull yourself together.'

She shook her head. 'There's no point to any of this. Why look for Jimmy, now? It's a long way to the bottom of the glen. We should leave before dark.'

Warwick shook his head. 'I know a way out from down there, so we won't have to climb up here again. I'm going whether you want to or not. I want that ring back.'

He started along the path, beckoning to her. 'Come on, it won't take long.'

Mallory limped behind him as the sky turn deep purple and the dusk deepened into twilight. Anger boiled in her. Sam was gone and they were in danger of getting caught in the mountains for the night, but all her father could think about was the stupid ring.

Her tears started to stream down her cheeks again as

the bleak reality of the situation hit her. Her father snorted in disgust at her tears, and said, 'I'm honestly surprised you've lasted so long in this game, hen. You shouldn't let your emotions rule.'

Warwick stopped when they reached the bottom of the glen. He looked up at the steep mountain, checking the position of the slope where Jimmy and Mallory had fallen. 'Wait here. I won't be long.'

Mallory sat down on a fallen tree. Her body ached and grief threatened to overwhelm her. There didn't seem to be any point in arguing with her father anymore. She closed her eyes and listened to the sounds of her father pushing through the bracken at the bottom of the slope.

~

Warwick shoved through sharp branches, wincing as they poked and scratched his face. The going was hard in the darkness, but despite the rough terrain and thick forest, he remained focused on the point below the shale drop, finally breaking through to a rocky clearing at the bottom. He sniffed at the metallic smell of blood in the air and pulled a flashlight out of his pocket, shining it on the rocks at the bottom of the cliff. Dark blood stains on the rocks led from the centre of the clearing into the forest. He clicked the torch off, waited for his eyes to adjust to the dark and cocked his head, but no sounds emanated from the forest. He moved in cautious silence toward the area where the blood stains led and stopped momentarily when he saw the dark shape of his brother in a clearing on the floor of the forest. He walked toward him, his entire body tense and alert, but the shape remained motionless. He stopped and stared down at his brother for a full minute, his face devoid of emotion, before pushing him with the toe of his boot. Jimmy moaned, the sound so low that it would have gone unnoticed if the forest wasn't so quiet.

Warwick squatted down and stared into the face of his brother. Jimmy's eyes fluttered open and he returned his brother's gaze with an unfocused stare.

'You're dying, wee Jimmy.' Warwick reached toward Jimmy's hand. 'It's my turn again, and guess what? I get to take if off your nearly dead hand.'

He grabbed Jimmy's hand, grinning as he started to twist the ring off his finger. Jimmy tried to pull his hand away and let out a howling gurgle.

Warwick looked at Jimmy's wounded ribs, noticed that the bleeding was slowing to a trickle and nodded with satisfaction. 'She's a good girl, Mallory. Has more of her old man in her than we realised. You probably should have killed her when you had the chance.' He stood up. 'I've never raised a hand against you, and I won't start now. I think we can both agree you're not getting out of here alive, anyway. Goodbye, little brother.'

~

Back in the clearing, Mallory sat up at the sound of a faint howl, suddenly alert in the silent darkness that followed. The skin on the back of her neck prickled. It felt as though the dead may walk at night here, perhaps take their revenge on those who still lived. The thought that Jimmy may have survived, may have killed her father while she waited here and was possibly approaching at that very moment, filled her with dread. She stood up and looked around the small clearing. Nothing moved, but faint noises emanated from the forest. She backed up against a tree opposite the direction of the noises and strained to hear. A faint crackle sounded at the edge of the forest and her heart rate accelerated.

Her father appeared in front of her, seemingly out of nowhere. She jumped, throwing her arms up, braced in readiness to attack and defend.

Warwick halted and then moved backwards, his movements jittery. 'Easy girl.' He stared past her toward the forest. 'Let's get out of here.'

'Did you find Jimmy?' she asked.

'No. The ring is gone,' he said, his voice strained and hoarse.

Mallory tried to read his expression, but he averted his face and a shudder passed through him, as if he were about to cry.

Weariness and despair gripped her. Sam was dead and her father was grieving over a useless ring that was lost in the Highlands. He didn't seem to care that his brother was out there somewhere, wounded and most likely dying. A tight wave of anger moved through her chest. Her father was not the man she remembered, and Jimmy the Cat was not the uncle she wanted. It was all too much to take in, but she realised people had made the connection long before she had.

She stared into the darkness of the forest one last time. 'What if he's still alive?'

Warwick patted her arm and she winced internally against his touch but kept herself still.

'I'll come back tomorrow, lass. But he probably won't survive the night.'

She stared into the accusatory darkness of the forest. It

was silent, still. It seemed to tell her that she should have tried harder – should have gone to Sam's aid. She turned away, following her father along the path that snaked upwards out of the glen. As far as she could tell, Sam was dead, she couldn't trust her father and Jimmy had nine lives. Her uncle's disappearance was one more thing to worry about, because she knew she was still in Trafford's sights.

~

The man pushed the barrow along the narrow track between the pines, stopping to inspect a growth of wild mushrooms in the morning light. He bent over, running his fingers lightly across the velvet tops of the fungi as he squinted into the soft, dawn fog wisping through the forest like a ghost.

'There be some good ones here, hen,' he called to the woman behind him.

She came toward him, her movements slow and cautious due to a combination of the rough forest floor and the biting arthritis in her knees, hips and hands. When she reached him, she stopped for a moment, leaning on her knees to catch her breath, before nodding appreciatively at the mushrooms. The pair set to work, picking the fungi in companionable silence. After they finished, they kept moving along the narrow track, their eyes focused on the ground, as they searched for more of the coveted Porcini and Boletes. The man stopped when he reached the edge of a clearing and leant against a pine tree while he waited for his wife to catch up again.

He smiled as she approached. 'Let's get to our usual spot, hen. Then we can take a break, have a nice cup of tea.'

He started to push the barrow toward a large flat tree

stump when he noticed a dark lump on the ground toward the cliffside of the clearing. He frowned. Whatever the object was, it didn't fit into the landscape. It wasn't the carcass of a deer. It was too big and long to be a wild pig, and there hadn't been wolves or bears in this forest since before his father's time. He stared harder, his eyes widening as realisation hit.

'Hen!'

The woman heard the hoarse urgency in her husband's voice and increased her pace as much as her aching joints allowed. She came up beside him, her eye following to where he pointed.

'It be a body, hen.'

She nodded. 'Could have come undone on the trails above, perhaps?' She rubbed her swollen knuckles and blew warm air into her palms. 'It happens a bit.'

He frowned. 'True that… but come now, we have never seen a body in this glen before! Not many people venture here, hen. It's not on any tourist guides, and the locals, well—' He stopped and swept a hand toward the coast, toward the Cameron land they knew to avoid.

She nodded, glancing back into the forest, her lips compressed as if to hold back words that may incriminate.

They looked at each other for a moment, before starting toward the body. They hesitated at the same time, looking to each other again for support, both suddenly aware of the deep silence in the glen. The woman shivered involuntarily and swayed toward her husband. When they stopped near the body, they took each other's hands and stared at the man on the ground. His head was rotated to one side at an uncomfortable angle, his face turned almost into the ground, revealing a deep gash that ran from the top of his head down the side of his neck. Dried blood surrounded the upper half of his body. The lower half was twisted in the opposite direction, legs splayed over each other, boots scuffed and dirty, as though he had tried to run without success.

The woman bent over and touched the man's hand. It was icy cold, clammy to the touch. She withdrew her hand, wiping it on her skirt.

'He's already gone,' she whispered, crossing herself as she cast a superstitious eye skyward.

'Aye. But we'll not be leaving him here, hen.'

She shivered again. They had found hikers before, but this one was different. They found them in one of the usual glens for hikers. This glen was off the maps. Locals wouldn't risk coming here, surely no one would, unless they were involved with the Camerons. She stared at the man's prone body. He was wearing an expensive suit. Who wore a suit in the Highlands? His boots were polished to such a degree that, despite the scuffs and dirt, she could see the tree line reflected on the glossy patches across the toes. She crossed herself again. She didn't want to touch the dead body again, didn't want to be responsible for whatever damnation touching the dead man might bring her way.

Her husband knelt and stared at the silent form. He took a deep breath. 'We have to take a proper look to be sure.'

She screeched, 'To be sure?' She clapped a hand over her mouth as the sound reverberated in the silence. 'Sorry my love, I'm feart.'

Her husband nodded. 'I ken. It's not every day we have

to deal with the likes of this.' He glanced at the body and scratched his head. 'But we need to see if he's got any life left in him.' He reached out, rolled the man over and gasped, his eyes widening in fright. 'Well now! How is this even possible, hen? It's wee Jimmy.'

His wife leant forward, peering over her husband's shoulder, her face taut with terror. 'Aye, it's nae possible, yet here he is.' She straightened, shaking her head, and repeated, 'It's nae possible. How would he be getting here, then?'

They straightened and stepped away together, both studying the dead man for a moment, both aware of the dangerous implications of their find.

'We must leave him here, Callum,' the wife whispered. 'There's foul play in this, to be sure. We'll not help ourselves by getting involved.'

'Wait, we cannae do that, Janey.' He stood and walked back to the barrow. 'Highland men deserve a proper burial, even this one.' He wheeled the barrow over to the prone body and handed the woman the basket full of mushrooms.

She spat on the ground near the prone body. 'Not this one, Callum. Dying in the Highlands is more than he deserves. He cannae hope to rest in peace as well.'

Callum stepped forward, placing a gentle hand over her mouth. 'Hush, Janey. The mountains have ears. People have died for less.'

He gathered himself again and dropped on one knee, sliding his arms under Jimmy's shoulders and heaved him toward the barrow.

Jimmy let out a low moan and the couple froze.

Callum let go and Jimmy's body slumped to the ground. 'I thought you said he were dead, love?'

'Aye and I thought you said he were too!' Janey cried, her eyes wild.

'We have to stay calm now,' he said. He clenched his jaw and grabbed Jimmy, feeling his limbs. He pushed one of Jimmy's arms onto his chest and frowned. 'If he's alive it's barely. He's cold as ice, going stiff, and I can't feel a breath. He'll not be causing us any trouble.'

She shook her head and waved frantic hands at the trees beyond the clearing. 'That moan, it were just air escaping. But what if it were his spirit.' Her voice rose in panic. 'I don't want his spirit following us home, Callum. What would we be doing with him? Where could we go to escape?'

'We can worry about that later, hen.'

She grabbed his arm. 'What if we're found with him? Think about it! If his body is found at our bothy, we won't have to worry about anything later!'

The couple stood over Jimmy, staring at each other in the silence without speaking.

Jimmy let out another low moan and Janey tightened her grip on his arm. 'He's not our problem, Callum. None of that clan has ever been our problem. Let's keep it that way.'

He shook off her grip and slid the point of his boot under Jimmy's ribs, lifting the side of his body slightly off the ground. There was no resistance or sound. He moved his foot and the body dropped back onto the ground. Callum nodded to himself, convinced the sound they had heard earlier was due to moving the body for the first time. He started to sweat and wiped the moisture from his forehead. He stared at the corpse and cursed. He didn't want to be the one to find this lad in the glen.

He looked at Janey, his expression mirroring his internal struggle. 'We can't leave a Highland man, hen.'

She shook her head. 'He's not been a Highland man for years and then some. Look at those clothes.' She snorted. 'Aye, only the best for this lad and all, eh?' She stepped away, her tone decisive. 'He's dead. He's not our kin. He's not our problem, Callum.' She stepped toward her husband, grabbing his hand in hers. 'Come on, man, he's never been one of us and he certainly isnae one of us just now.'

Callum ran a hand through his hair and, despite his reluctance, nodded agreement. He wouldn't touch the lad again. He turned away without another word and made his way back to the barrow, aware of his wife following like a silent shadow.

The couple stood either side of the barrow, listening to the unnatural silence settling over the forest.

'What's happened to the birds, hen?' Callum whispered.

'What if the banshees are coming to bring him back?' she whispered.

'Dinnae talk that superstition,' he whispered in reply.

The hairs prickled on the back of his neck for a moment. He wanted to suggest they do a requiem of sorts for the fallen lad, but memories surfaced of a time long ago, standing over his father's grave. His father who was only thirty-five at the time. Who hadn't deserved to die so young. His father didn't get to choose when he died because of this lad's clan. A decent burial was more than the bastard lying in the glen deserved.

He crossed himself, his eyes to the sky, and asked his father's spirit for forgiveness. He stayed there, waiting until a decent amount of time had passed before reaching out to

Janey and breaking the spell. 'Come on, hen. He's not going anywhere.'

She nodded. 'I don't want to look for more mushrooms today, Cal.'

He nodded. They turned away from the cliffs and Jimmy's body, walking back into the depths of the forest, with the only sound the trundling wheel on the wooden barrow.

When the couple reached their bothy, they emptied the barrow and sorted the mushrooms on the scrubbed wooden table in the kitchen.

Callum sat down suddenly and pressed his fingers into his eyes. 'I feel like I should go back. It don't seem right leaving a man – even one of them – out there and all.'

Janey's eyes widened in fear. 'For the love of our clan, we cannae even say his name out loud. I dinnae want his body here.'

He shook his head. 'Aye, but he needs a burial. I guess I should attend to it in the morning.'

She shook her head. 'You'll not. There'll be no going back to that glen until his spirit has passed over. You'll not give him the Sitting and Lykewake. He dinnae deserve such attentions to see him on his journey.' Her lip curled. 'We both know where he's headed.'

She turned her back on her husband, indicating that the matter was closed. She wanted no part of it, and wished with all of her heart that they had never found Jimmy Cameron in their glen.

9

MALLORY stared at the glassy surface of the loch as they returned to Warwick's bothy. She had so many questions for her father, especially about the Topaz Stallion, but she couldn't bring herself to begin. Tears pressed at the back of her eyes. It seemed impossible to her that Sam was gone forever. The night in Bruges returned, the feelings it evoked cutting through her chest like a knife. She had hoped they would find a way to have many more of those nights together, that the connection they felt would grow until there would be no questions and no doubts. She had to admit that she had secretly hoped Sam would find a way to fit her into his life and leave the law behind forever. The future looked pointless, now. Where would she go, what would she do to fill the void he had left? Her chest clenched. There was no Sam anymore. She would never again see his green eyes sparkling and the flash of his grin after he told a joke, or feel the warmth of his arms wrapped around her. Cold fear gripped her. She was truly alone in the world and still in danger from Trafford and Eve. Tears rolled silently down her cheeks as the sun started to drop, causing the shadows to lengthen like long, grasping fingers over the

194

calm surface of the loch.

Warwick reached out a hand and squeezed her shoulder. 'Don't cry, lass. He wouldn't want that.'

She shook his hand off and turned on him. 'You didn't even like him because he was a lawman.' Her voice started to rise. 'And you didn't know him at all! How the hell would you know what he wanted?'

Warwick looked at her for a moment, his expression hurt. 'What matters to me is you. If you wanted to be with a lawman, I would accept your choice.' He shook his head. 'Anyway, that's a pointless line of thought now. It's more important to make sure you're safe.'

He slowed as they reached the area near the bothy. 'Some things are not always black and white. Especially in love.' He glanced at her, his expression guarded. 'It's a good thing you understand that, now.' He glanced in the rear and side mirrors. 'Tell me, you do understand that?'

She frowned. 'What do you mean?'

He geared down as they turned onto the narrow track that led back to the bothy. 'Well, matters of the heart are complex, lass.'

Mallory frowned. Something in his tone seemed off, almost manipulative, as if he were trying to direct her mind in a particular direction.

'Is there something you're trying to tell me?' she asked.

When they rolled to halt in front of the bothy, he shook his head, staring straight ahead. 'No. You'll see soon enough.'

She followed his gaze and saw the door of the bothy open. Iona stepped out into the sunshine, a broad smile on her face. Mallory looked at her for a moment without registering what she meant to the conversation. She looked at her father.

He sat completely still, a red flush creeping up his neck and across his cheeks. 'We're married, lass. We've been married almost ten years.'

The information hit Mallory like a fist in the stomach. In the almost fifteen years he'd been missing, she'd imagined him hiding, alone, lonely, and thinking only about how he could get back to his family. But for most of that time, he'd been playing house with this woman. She glared at Iona through the windscreen. 'Was she even legal ten years ago?'

Warwick's jaw clenched and his knuckles whitened as he continued to grip the steering wheel. 'It pains me to see your ideals broken, Mally, but adult relationships... well, they're complicated.'

She snorted. 'Don't give me that crap. I think I understand adult relationships well enough, thank you.'

He looked at her, his eyes hard. 'Really? You put your trust in a piece of scum like Derek James more than once. Then you take up with a lawman who will always choose the establishment over you.' He shook his head. 'You thought love would conquer all, didn't you? You thought a lawman would choose you over his duty.' He let out a dry snort of laughter. 'You don't know the first thing about the human condition.'

Her eyes widened. 'How do you know about Derek?'

He smiled and patted her leg, ignoring her attempt to flinch away. 'I've always kept tabs on you. You are my daughter.'

A rush of pain and anger engulfed her, making her throat close. She knew she was close to screaming and howling like the wounded child she felt was still trapped inside of her.

She opened her door and stared at Iona. The full import of her father's words slammed into her.

She turned back to her father and yelled, 'You left your family for a younger woman, you piece of shit!' She jumped out of the vehicle. 'Niall was right! You were never worth the breath it took to say your name.'

He flapped an irritable hand at her. 'Don't be so dramatic, lass. It's not that simple! Love can't be denied. You know that.'

'Oh, come on! What about the love for your family? What about—' She stopped, her look of shock quickly replaced by a sneer. 'What about the fact that you've never divorced mum? How could you, even? You would have been found!'

Warwick interrupted as he climbed out of the vehicle, slamming his door. 'The logistics of my life are not your concern. Don't forget I was trying to protect you.'

She snorted. 'Yeah, right! Mum went to her grave eating her heart out, thinking you'd died in a terrible accident. Thinking you would find a way to return if you were alive. Meanwhile you were sitting in the Scottish Highlands the whole time, getting it on with your *wee lassie*!'

'Warwick?' Iona's voice cut through their conversation, the hurt tone in her voice failing to cover the steel below. 'You said you were already divorced.'

A flash of anger passed over his face. 'Go back into the bothy, woman!' He stepped toward her and pointed at the closed door, the threat obvious.

She shook her head and opened her mouth to speak, but he waved at her to be quiet before turning back to Mallory. 'Do you think you would have had a normal childhood? Do you think Niall would be a doctor if you'd been on the run with me?' His face softened and smiled. 'Come on, lass, I would have done more harm in staying.' He moved toward her as she slammed the door of the vehicle, shepherding her inside the bothy with quiet insistence, talking about the precious family memories he held, in a tone mellow with nostalgia.

Mallory felt her resolve waver for a moment in the face of his logic. Perhaps he had saved them from a life of hardship and worry. She looked around the bothy at the expensive artwork, the rows of single malts on the bar, the silk throws on the plush sofa, the intricate sculptures and the view over the loch and her resolve hardened.

'You haven't exactly suffered. I've no doubt you could have sent us to a boarding school, and you and mum would have been safe here.'

'No, you're wrong, lass. If Jimmy had ever suspected that I had any interest in you, he would have come after you. As it was, he kept an eye on you, but he didn't bother to act because I wasn't in the picture. I was protecting you from the suffering he would have caused.' He scratched irritably at the stubble on his chin. 'Why do you think he took the time to find you in Australia, yet didn't kill you? He wanted to use you against me.'

She stepped forward, her eyes darkening. 'Don't make this about Jimmy – he's nothing to me. When you left, we did suffer! We were poor and Mum was always sad and broken. Our childhood was anything but bloody normal anyway, so why leave in the middle of it? Why not face whatever came at us together?'

He sighed. 'You don't understand! Look, lass, what's done is done. There's no point hurling accusations and recriminations now. We must focus on the matter at hand.'

She folded her arms. 'So that's it. Just move on like everything is fine. I can't do that.'

Warwick raised a hand, his voice hard. 'Enough! If we remain distracted by the past, we end up in big trouble right now.'

'As usual, you worry about yourself.' Mallory's voice broke. 'You don't care that Sam died trying to do the right thing, trying to protect me from Jimmy and Trafford. You don't care that I've been looking for you all of my adult life. All you care about is that stupid ring!'

Hurt and anger boiled inside Mallory. She didn't know how to voice the confusion and pain she felt, and it seemed her father wouldn't care if she did. 'I doubt you would even consider my safety if you still had the ring. I'd bet good money you'd sell me out to protect the Topaz Stallion if it were still in your possession.'

Warwick snorted, unconsciously covering the bare pinkie where the ring had once been with his other hand. 'You need me more than I need you, lass. Don't forget that.'

She shook her head and turned on her heel, intent on leaving him to whatever mess awaited him.

He came after her, stopping her at the door. 'Mal, please. You can't walk out of here without a plan. You've no protection on either side now. You would never make it out of the country alive on your own.' He touched her arm softly. 'And what if the authorities get hold of you – do you honestly think they would believe that you had nothing to do with Sam's death?' Unshed tears welled in his eyes. 'Please lass, if you get caught by the Heat, Trafford will have you killed before you leave the holding cell.'

He took hold of her arm, rubbing it affectionately. 'Believe me, even if I had the ring, giving it to him would not help to protect you.'

She remained rigid and shrugged his hand off her arm. 'That stupid ring is responsible for Sam's death.'

He sighed. 'The ring is gone and so is the lawman. Let the past stay where it is and listen to me. I'm going to send it out into the network that Jimmy killed you and the lawman. That is the only way you will be safe.'

She shrugged. It was all too much. Sam was gone forever. She would never feel his arms around her again. It really didn't matter where she went.

'Mallory?' Warwick said, his voice tense. 'I'll make sure your death is accepted. You know what you must do.'

She opened the door and looked back at her father for a moment. He seemed completely different to her. He looked like a cunning old man who would sell his grandmother to the highest bidder. The glamour she had nursed in her memories was well and truly destroyed.

'I never stopped looking for you. I dreamed of the day I would find you.' She shook her head. 'But I don't know who you are. Do whatever you need to do. I am better off dead, anyway.'

He stepped forward. 'Honey, you can't go out into the world as yourself. You will be dead in less than forty-eight hours. What will that prove?' He smiled, his eyes soft.

'Come on, lass. I never claimed to be a saint, but I do care about you. I have plenty of things in the dressing room you can use.' He moved to one side and gestured toward a closed door near the kitchen. 'Go on lass, please. Do your magic and disappear. I'll take care of the rest.'

10

WARWICK slid the curtain aside and peered into the falling dusk outside. He could still make out Mallory's figure hiking along the path toward the main road. When she finally disappeared behind the trees, he dropped the curtain and turned to Iona. 'We have to pack.'

Iona stared at him, her eyes wide. 'Pack?'

He nodded, lifting artwork off the walls as he spoke. 'Trafford will find this place. It's only a matter of time, and I don't think we have much of that left.'

He stopped for a moment and turned to take her face between his hands. 'He probably already knows where we are.' He kissed her forehead and pulled her closer for a moment. 'I can't risk anything happening to you, my love. Trafford will come after me, looking for the Stallion.'

'But it is lost,' she said.

'Trafford wouldn't believe that story, and besides…' He smiled and winked as he slid his hand into his coat pocket. He withdrew his hand, palm upwards. The ring glinted under the soft lights of the bothy. He smiled again as he slipped it onto his pinkie. 'It was never lost. You know I wouldn't leave it behind.'

Her eyes widened. 'But, Jimmy?'

He stepped away, his face guarded. 'I had to leave him behind as well. He was badly injured, close to death. There's no way he will survive a night in the open up here. Believe me, that is the best outcome for everyone, Jimmy included.' He stared out the window, avoiding her gaze. 'My brother never did know when to stop.' He paused for a moment, his eyes narrowing. 'And the same goes for that lawman. He won't last long out there either; exposure will finish the job.'

She gasped. 'But—but I thought you said he… you lied to your own daughter. The lawman is not dead?'

He frowned. 'He's as good as – it's just a matter of time He won't survive the night.' He pushed her away gently. 'Imagine if I had attempted to save him? Think about what that would have done to my daughter, yes?'

She stepped backwards, shaking her head. 'Restored her trust in you, perhaps?'

'There are some things you do not understand,' he growled. 'It's better this way, trust me.' He turned his back, indicating the conversation was over, and moved toward a dresser, pulling open drawers and upending them on the sofa. 'Enough chat, now. We have limited time.'

He started sorting through the jumble of papers and trinkets. 'I don't mean to imply that my brother's passing makes me happy.' He shook his head and looked forlorn. 'Of course it doesn't, but now that Jimmy is gone we can return to Abrigada. He was the only one who knew about the property in Portugal.' He smiled at Iona. 'Come on, hen. You can go home. We'll be safe there now.'

She frowned. 'Why did he never look for you here? It was your family home, no?'

He shook his head. 'Not this bothy. He didn't know about this one. This is on the last edge of Cameron land. I built this bothy years after we'd both sworn we would never return. The original Cameron bothy is on the other side of the mountain.' He chuckled. 'Jimmy would have checked there for sure, but maybe he didn't think I would have the balls to return to Scotland without him.' He stopped to scratch his chin, his face pensive. 'Or perhaps he simply could not find me. I've always been the smarter one.'

Iona stared at him without answering, a small tic jumping near her left temple.

He started searching through the papers again, looking up with a megawatt smile that he knew would disarm her. 'Don't worry, my love. You are different. I will always look after you first.'

The pair fell silent as they worked feverishly, packing suitcases and boxes with trinkets, art, books and personal belongings. Warwick went outside and backed the Range Rover up to the bothy door, and the pair loaded the suitcases and boxes into the back of the vehicle in silence. When they finished packing the car, they did a last sweep of the property. Warwick nodded, satisfied that there was nothing left that could lead Trafford to him. The pair stopped in the main room in front of the picture window that looked out over the loch.

Warwick stood behind Iona and took her in his arms, resting his chin on her shoulder. 'It's a beautiful view, my lovely. I'll miss it.' He tightened his arms. 'But we are together, and that is what counts.'

He felt her body start to shake and realised she was crying. 'Don't cry, my darling, we've had many wonderful years here, we've lost nothing. And we will always have each other. There will be plenty more memories to make in Portugal.'

Iona nodded and reached back to cup his cheek in her hand. He kissed her neck, working his way up toward her face until she turned her head to meet his lips. They remained locked in their silent embrace until a loud crash behind them broke the spell. Warwick spun toward the noise, letting out a grunt of surprise at the sight of Sam Walker standing in the doorway.

Sam leant against the jamb, his breathing laboured. 'I'm guessing you didn't think you'd see me again after you and your daughter left me to die alone on the mountain?'

Iona said, 'Wait, Mallory did—'

Warwick gripped her hand, crushing the bones together in his haste to silence her. 'I can't believe you would doubt my daughter's feelings for you. Do you honestly think she would leave you behind if she had a choice?' He glared at Sam. 'Lawmen are the same, no matter where they come from. Only thinking about themselves and their precious rules,' he said, his voice dripping with contempt. 'Mallory didn't help you because she is dead.'

Sam slumped against the jamb, his face pale. 'But how… how is that even possible?'

'My brother attacked you and killed her. You know what he is like. It all happened so fast, son. There was nothing I could do.'

Sam sagged against the doorway and pressed a hand to his temple. 'You should have stopped him.'

Warwick realised Sam was still carrying pain from the injury to his head.

He put his arm around Iona's waist, tears welling in his eyes. 'You don't think I know that? You don't think I tried?' His shoulders slumped. 'Believe me, I tried, but I am an old man. I have been out of this game for years. Do you really think I could outgun Jimmy?'

Sam shrugged and pushed away from the jamb. 'I don't know what to think.' His eyes darkened. 'But you know I still intend to take you in.' He nodded toward Warwick's hand. 'And return the ring that you have miraculously managed to keep, despite being unable to help your daughter.'

Warwick covered his pinkie for a moment and then shrugged, his tears gone as quickly as they had appeared. 'And how do you propose to do that, now?' He moved toward Sam, his eyes appraising. 'You're unarmed and injured.' He smiled again, exposing his teeth to the gums. 'I am not inclined to do what you ask.'

Sam straightened, blocking the doorway. 'I reckon your daughter really didn't know you at all.'

Warwick's eyes flashed. 'Mallory's knowledge of me is none of your business.' He moved with sudden swiftness, but Sam dropped as the older man lunged, grabbing his arm as he swung it at him, and spinning him against the wall. Warwick snarled as Sam grappled with his free arm, twisting it behind his back and forcing his body flat against the wall.

Behind them, forgotten by Sam, Iona lifted a paperweight from the desk and moved silently across the room. She drew back her arm and slammed the weight into the back of Sam's head. The wet crunch of heavy glass on bone made her squeal and drop the paperweight as Sam slumped to the ground.

Warwick spun around to her, his eyes hot and wild. 'Well done, my lass!' He grabbed her by the wrist, planting a hard kiss on her lips. 'Now, let's get out of here.' He moved to the window and peered into the darkened forest outside. 'It's like bloody central station here today. Trafford could arrive at any moment.'

She hesitated and looked down at Sam. 'What about him?'

Warwick looked at him, lying motionless near the door. 'He surely cannot be that tough. That's the second hit he's taken to the head today, and he's not dressed in the right gear to withstand a night up here.' He glanced outside at the lengthening darkness grasping the last of the light. 'There's not much chance of him getting help if he does come around.'

He squatted beside Sam, rolling his body back and forth as he pulled his jacket off and searched the pockets. He threw it into a corner before patting down his body. 'No phone.'

'What about his wallet?' Iona asked.

He shrugged. 'Leave it.' He tugged at her arm. 'Come on, my love, don't worry about him dying a slow death. You know how cold it gets here without a fire. He won't feel his life slipping away. And if he's still alive when the goons get here, Trafford will give him a quick finish.'

The couple grabbed the last of their belongings and stepped over Sam, leaving the door to the bothy open as they ran toward the vehicle. Warwick gunned the motor and roared down the track toward the road, the bellow of the engine echoing over the glen as darkness fell over the bothy.

~

Sam woke, disoriented and unsure of where he was. He stayed still, rolling his eyes to take in his surroundings. He looked at the floorboards near his face and followed the line of the timber to a wall. Except for weak moonlight coming through a large window, the bothy was in darkness and the floor under him as frigid as the air in the room. His limbs were stiff from the cold. He couldn't feel his toes. He knew he had to move soon or die. He turned his head slowly, and groaned as pain spread from the wound on the back of his head, and joined the throb in his temples before travelling the length of his spine.

Memories of the earlier confrontation with Warwick returned to him. His mind reeled back over the day, his heart lurching at the thought of Mallory's death. Not even twelve hours ago, he'd been in her father's car with her, ready to protect her with his life. He remembered her looking back at him from the front seat and squeezed his eyes shut. Her passing was too sudden, surreal almost. Fragments of the night in Bruges returned, the sweetness of the images causing his grief to intensify. It was more than he could bear. His limbs, heart and head felt cold and heavy. The thought of never seeing her again sat on him, the heft of it settling on his chest. It was tempting to stay where he was and let the freezing night take him.

He closed his eyes, surrendering to despair. His heart slowed and his breathing became shallow as his thoughts spun away, back to long afternoons hunting lizards in the saltbush with his father while parrots wheeled and flashed in a rainbow of colours across the sky. The smell of campfire smoke drifted on the lazy heated air with the quiet singsong of his father's voice. He smiled, his breathing becoming shallower as he drifted back into a time of stories and dreams.

His father's voice stopped its lulling chant. He felt his hand on his shoulder, heard him whisper in his ear, 'No son, this is not your time or place to die.'

Sam's eyes snapped open. Of course, his father wasn't with him, but he felt the spirit connection all the same, felt the pull to return to his body and face the situation like the man his father had taught him to be. He moved his arms and legs, trying to get feeling back into his extremities. His eyes wandered the darkened room while he waited for sensation to return to his hands and feet, and he wondered for a moment if, despite his father's message, this would be the last place he saw on earth.

A gust of icy air moved over him and he realised the bothy door was wide open. He rolled his head toward it and stared at the stars twinkling in the clear velvet sky outside the door, their beauty overwhelming against his current grief. Tears ran in hot tracks down his face, but he fought back against the overwhelming urge to remain locked in hopelessness. If he gave in now, he would die alone on this frigid floor. He would be taken by the cold, grey night into the spirit world of a foreign land. He felt his heart begin to thud. He couldn't let himself die here. He would never see the country he loved again if he didn't make himself move and find a way to get warm. He rolled onto his side, groaning as the pounding in his head intensified and his stomach started performing sickening flips. He moved his arms and legs, then pushed himself up into a seated position, panting as the thudding engulfed his entire body and his stomach started churning faster. After a moment he stood up and slid, with both hands flat for balance, along the wall.

When he found a light switch, he flicked it on, squinting against the blinding light. As his vision slowly adjusted, he froze at the sight of a man's silhouette in the doorway of the bothy. The man lifted an arm, and Sam saw the shape of the gun in his hand.

The man gave a tight smile. 'A little birdie sent us,' he said.

He stepped inside the doorway. 'Away from the wall, and put those hands where I can see them, my man.'

Sam raised his arms, aware that the pulsing ache in his body and the blood roaring in his ears were making him feel dizzy. He stared at the man, taking in the sharp suit, polished shoes and slicked down hair. Maybe one of Trafford's goons, but something about him seemed wrong – more law than outlaw. Sam felt a glimmer of hope even though his raised arms felt like lead and his shoulders burned. He forced a smile and tried to relax his body so he looked as non-threatening as possible. Another wave of dizziness passed through him. He stepped back, hoping to find the solidity of the wall, but the roaring in his ears increased to such a level that he barely heard the click of the safety being cocked on the gun before the world tilted and went black.

11

SAM woke to the sound of electronic beeping and hushed voices. He stared at the ceiling while he waited for his mind and body to reconnect. The ceiling and walls were white, sterile, and the mattress he lay on was firm, the sheets crisp and tightly wrapped around his body. His mind returned for a moment to his near-death experience on the cold floor of the bothy, and the stranger in the doorway with the gun. He gave silent thanks that he was alive and felt a sudden tug of homesickness for drifts of red dust beneath his feet, and the pressing heat from endless skies of white-blue. He fancied he could smell wattle and gum, hear croaking frogs in a damp billabong dusk, and see his father squatted over a campfire at the Breakaways, turning the coals as stars began to prick the sky above.

'Thank you, old fella. I owe you one,' he whispered, as a deeper wave of homesickness rolled through his body, settling in his chest like a stone. He rolled his head to the right and saw a drip in his arm leading up to the beeping machine. He heard a door open to his left and turned to see a man in a suit step inside the room.

Sam gave a slight nod and heard him mutter, 'Bloody Aussies,' as he approached the bed.

Jervis stared down at Sam. 'Do you remember me, son? From special ops? You gave us a bit of a turn, but it looks like I won't have to fill out more paperwork explaining your demise.' He paused, his expression appraising. 'So that's something.'

Sam smiled and Jervis grinned in return. 'I'm glad I sent the boys in when I did. We all thought you were on a flogging to nowhere, but it seems we were wrong.' He ran a hand across his forehead, his expression suddenly tired. 'We'll need a debrief on your side when you're feeling up to it.'

He looked at his watch and back at Sam. 'Oh, and you'll be wanting the latest on Warwick Cash, no doubt. I'm afraid it's not good news at all.'

A tide of anger rose in Sam at the thought of Warwick. If Mallory could have seen the kind of person her father really was, perhaps the worst of the situation could have been avoided. Instead, she had trusted her father, and it had cost her her life.

Jervis stepped back from the bed, as if aware he needed to give Sam time to process. He cleared his throat, his expression sympathetic. 'He's gone to ground. He managed to get out of the country via the ferry to Ireland. We traced him to Derry and then lost him. We believe he's already in Europe. He knows how to stay hidden.' He shook his head. 'We won't give up, but given his track record, we honestly don't expect to catch him quickly.'

Sam sighed. 'Yeah, I know what he's like.' He lifted his arm and pointed at the drip. 'As soon as I get the word from the doc, I'll take you back to the Highlands. There's evidence at the bothy.' He paused for a moment. 'You will need to take backup. Jimmy Contanti may still be out there, somewhere in the mountains.'

Jervis shook his head. 'I seriously doubt that, old man. There's talk on the grapevine that Jimmy the Cat is dead.'

Sam's eyes widened in disbelief. 'That's impossible. He's like a Schrödinger's Cat!'

Jervis chuckled. 'Some of the chat is coming from reputable sources. It seems Warwick made sure the Cat reached his ninth life.'

Sam frowned. It seemed impossible that Jimmy could be dead. 'But he's the one that attacked me up there. He killed Mallory Cash.'

Jervis went still. 'Are you sure of that?'

'Warwick told me before he got the jump on me.' Sam frowned. 'There was someone else with him at the bothy.'

'Really? We're certain Warwick killed Jimmy, and it does make more sense if Jimmy killed his daughter now, doesn't it?'

Sam didn't answer. He wasn't certain he could talk about Mallory's death without revealing his feelings.

Jervis grabbed the notebook in his pocket and flipped it open. 'The other person at the bothy. Do you have a description?'

Sam shook his head. 'Not really. He was with a female, but I couldn't see her. She hit me from behind while I was subduing Warwick Cash.'

'Perhaps he lied to you. Perhaps it was his daughter who helped him escape.'

Sam shook his head. 'The woman had an accent I've

never heard before.'

Jervis frowned. 'You can't be certain it wasn't her if you didn't get a good look at her. She's a master at disguises, remember. It's possible she waited and attacked you when your back was turned.'

Sam closed his eyes. He wouldn't accept that Mallory would purposefully hurt him and leave him to die. He knew whoever was in the bothy with Warwick that night wasn't Mallory.

~

Sam sat in Jervis' office in Edinburgh, staring blindly out the window as fluffy clouds scudded across the soft-blue sky outside. The Scottish sky seemed smaller and closer than the one he was used to in the outback, the colours drawn from a different palette, but it was no less vivid. His gaze swept across the redbrick chimneys and up to the castle that overshadowed the city. The beauty of the place still managed to catch him out. It was a tamed beauty with the insistent touch of human organisation at its heart, so foreign to the country where he was born that it was fascinating to observe.

Jervis entered the room and sat down opposite Sam. He smiled and slid a file across the desk. 'Your super has been in touch.'

Sam nodded, ready to hear an acid-laced comment from his superior.

'He's awfully relieved that you've resurfaced. They thought they'd lost you forever.'

Sam felt a jolt of shock at the other man's words. He'd been so involved in the chase, so rolled up in his grief over Mallory, he'd failed to understand how the situation would appear to his Australian counterparts.

He smiled, wanting to make light of the situation. 'They should know I'm pretty hard to kill.'

Jervis smiled, but it didn't take the worry out of his eyes. 'We won't need you to go back to the Highlands. We've been back to the bothy since I spoke to you in the hospital. Trafford's men have definitely been there, too.'

He opened a file and shuffled through some papers. 'There has also been a connection to Eve Saldino nosing about, asking questions, which I must say we didn't expect and don't quite understand.' He looked up at Sam. 'But, there's no sign of Warwick, Jimmy or Mallory Cash, I'm afraid.'

He waited a moment, his expression sympathetic. 'We can only surmise at this point that they are either all hiding together, or that the reports are correct – Jimmy and Mallory are dead, and Warwick has gone to ground somewhere in Europe.'

Sam's heart sank. Eve Saldino was another problem, but there was no reason to believe she was a threat to him, and she could no longer threaten Mallory. He cast his mind through possible scenarios, but he couldn't see a reason for her involvement any more than he could imagine Mallory on the run with Jimmy. He wouldn't believe she had tried to kill him to help her father and uncle, but the alternative was even worse.

Jervis cleared his throat. 'We think it's best if you return home now, son. There's not much more you can help us with.'

He leant back in his chair, his mild tone belying Sam's sudden dismissal from the case. 'You've been a big help. We know that Warwick still has the ring because of you. We know there's a good chance Warwick is on the run with an unknown accomplice, and that Jimmy and Mallory Cash are probably dead.' He followed Sam's gaze to the sky outside, his expression pensive. 'Funny that despite us being able to connect Warwick and Jimmy as the Cameron brothers, we still have so many unknowns – your investigation has definitely helped answer some questions, and given us more to ponder.'

He turned back to the file, closing it as he continued to speak. 'Anyway, we also know that Trafford won't rest until he finds that ring. We'll keep a track on him, and he'll lead us to Warwick Cash in the end.'

EPILOGUE

THE planes of Eve's face softened momentarily as her daughter, Lily, approached the table. The hint of a patronising smile passed over her lips, replaced quickly by a hard, unyielding stillness.

Lily slid into the chair opposite and nodded. 'Mother.'

Eve snorted. 'Mother? Is that all you have to say?' She picked up her champagne flute, taking a measured sip. Her eyes locked on her daughter. Lily squirmed in her chair and refused to meet her mother's eyes.

Eve placed her glass on the table with delicate care. 'I'm waiting for an explanation.'

Lily drained her champagne and planted the glass on the table. 'I tracked the target to Scotland. Intelligence gathered on the mission suggested the target would travel to Mull of Kintyre.' Lily leant forward and refilled her glass with a shaking hand.

'Stop with all of the secret service bullshit,' Eve snapped. 'And?' She rapped her fingernails on the table, the staccato clack increasing with her obvious impatience.

'And she didn't arrive.'

'In other words, you were clumsy in your approach. She

detected you and gave you the slip.' She slammed her hand on the table, making the younger woman jump and spill her champagne. 'You think you know everything! It is a very good thing for you that you didn't cross Warwick's path. He would have killed you.' She glared at her daughter. 'You are a stupid, stupid girl.'

Lily's eyes narrowed. 'How so?'

Eve laughed. 'The fact that you even have to ask! Do you think I don't know what happened? Do you really think I need you to tell me?'

Lily reddened and stared at the table.

Eve slammed the table again. 'Look at me! You crossed paths with her twice in Bruges. That was two times too many.' She rolled her eyes. 'And what were you thinking, engaging in conversation with her? She would have been watching out for you after the second encounter. She sent you in the wrong direction.'

Lily's cheeks went a deeper shade of red and her eyes flashed. 'What about the lawman?'

'What about him?'

Lily felt her mother's eyes boring into her. Her entire face and neck flushed at the sound of Eve's brittle, barking laugh.

'Well, he is an attractive specimen, but don't you ever start getting a warm glow over a lawman or I will take you out myself!' Eve hissed into her glass and leant forward, her tone sharp. 'He was never the target, although I'm sure Trafford would have taken him out if he had the opportunity.' She raised an eyebrow at her daughter. 'Also, did you really think the lawman would be so bowled over by your beauty that he would forget what he is? He'd slap you behind bars in a heartbeat.' She leant forward, staring with a fresh intensity. 'What about Jimmy?'

Lily shrugged. 'He caught a train from London to Glasgow. From there he went to Fort William.' She frowned. 'Then he disappeared.'

'Did he see you?'

The young woman's gaze slid away from her mother. 'Word is, Trafford is looking for you.'

Eve waved a dismissive hand at her daughter. 'That's his problem because we both know he'll only find me once.'

Her mother leant closer to her. 'Did your father see you?'

Lily averted her face. 'What would it matter if he did? He wouldn't recognise me now.'

'Don't imagine that you can outwit a man like Jimmy. If he disappeared, it was intentional.'

Lily's bottom lip jutted out, and she glared at Eve. 'There's talk all over the place about Jimmy's death, you know. Everyone is saying Warwick killed him in the Highlands. And the Topaz Stallion – no one knows who has it now.'

Eve sat back holding her gaze as she folded her arms. 'Jimmy dead?' She shook her head. 'I would need to see it. You can't always believe the rumour mill.'

'I overheard one of Trafford's men talking about it.'

Eve snorted and upended her glass of champagne.

'And Jackson K confirmed.'

Eve's eyes widened momentarily. 'How would he come by that information?'

'He had someone on the ground up there, looking for Warwick. Word is, Jimmy was found beaten to death.'

Eve slumped back into her chair. Lily watched her, unsure if she should speak. The fleeting expressions passing across her mother's face were confusing. It was unclear whether she was happy or sad about the news.

Eve straightened. 'I should have done the job myself.'

Lily shifted in her seat. 'There's also talk that Mallory was killed by Jimmy.'

Eve sneered, her tone sardonic. 'Well, this has been a great result for the Cash family. Warwick gone, Mallory and Jimmy dead. One could be forgiven for thinking they are trying to get away from what they deserve.' She sipped her champagne and stared at her daughter through narrowed eyes. 'And you failed. You let her get away. If she is dead, I will never get my revenge.'

'I did my best, Mother.'

'Your best is always less than ordinary. I'll take it from here.'

'What do you intend to do?'

Eve's eyes widened. 'Do I detect concern? Is it possible you don't believe your little cousin is dead? Do you want to protect her from me?' She threw her head back and laughed. 'You really are monumentally stupid, girl! She's not capable of killing, but she would shop you to the Heat in a heartbeat.'

Eve stood and glared at her daughter. Lily looked down, her mouth set in a stubborn line as she twirled her glass in her hand and watched the bubbles whirlpool in the centre of the glass. She listened to the click of her mother's heels as she walked away and thought that maybe she was right, but also wrong. Perhaps she didn't really want to harm her cousin, and that's why she let her escape. And who knew?

Perhaps her cousin might care for her the way the father she'd never met and her cold-hearted mother had not? She smiled into her champagne. If there was a possibility Mallory was alive, perhaps she could find her and protect her from Eve. She liked the idea of having a real family, even if it was just one cousin.

~

The mounted police moved along the cordoned road in a neat line. Behind them, a royal carriage trundled in sedate elegance, a white gloved, slow-moving hand visible from the window. The crowd swelled as the carriage approached, the cheers and confetti lifting in colourful relief against the grey London skies above. The guards maintained their pace, with the odd snort or eye roll from their mounts. As they reached a narrow point in the road, a man in a heavy overcoat grabbed a young woman at the front of the crowd and rushed into the path of the trotting horses before the bobbies on the sidelines could stop him. He flashed a large knife as he did, and a panicked scream caused the crowd to contract and burst away from him in every direction. The guard barely broke rhythm as they approached, their hands firm on the restless mounts beneath them.

The young woman in the man's grasp dropped her shoulder, grabbed one of his arms and flipped him over her body. He landed with a thud and grunt in front of the guards, causing their horses to mill and half-rear in confusion, while the young woman turned and melted into the crowd without a backward glance. The mounted guards gathered their horses as the bobbies grappled with the winded man and cuffed him.

The captain of the guard called to a bobby, 'Get him

out of the way, man. We need to keep the carriage moving.'

The bobby pulled the man to the side of the road. As the horses passed, the captain asked, 'Where is the woman? Is she unharmed?'

The bobby scanned the confused, thinning crowd, but it was impossible. The woman had been wearing a black jacket and jeans in a crowd of people dressed similarly. She was nowhere to be seen. He shrugged and pushed the cuffed man toward a waiting car.

Within minutes, the footage flashed across screens around the globe and circulated on endless replay, as news outlets marvelled at the young woman's effortless removal of an attacker and the quick response of the British Police.

~

In a basement in London, Trafford frowned at the footage and hit the record button the next time the story ran. He rewound the footage and scrolled until the woman's face was visible on the frozen screen. He leant back, grinning in triumph, pointed a finger gun at the screen and whispered, 'Gotcha!'

~

At the same time, in a waterfront hotel in Monaco, Eve watched the television while she brushed her blonde hair into a tight bun and pulled a sleek red dress over her body. She moved closer to the screen above the dresser and watched replays of the woman throwing the man over her shoulder. On the third run through, she threw back her head and laughed out loud. She picked up her phone, clicked on a contact and typed, *the dead girl is still walking, but not for long.*

~

On the other side of the world in Australia, the footage

played endlessly in the Sydney operations room of the Federal Police. A group gathered, keen to study the response of the British police and royal guard to a possible terror attack. Each time they watched the woman throw the man in front of the horses, an appreciative cheer for the man's downfall went through the crowd. Sam entered the room and moved closer to the screen to watch the action. After the story completed a fourth loop, he felt his heart contract and his blood turn to burning ice in his veins.

There was no doubt in his mind: the woman on the screen was Mallory Cash.

To be continued...

ABOUT THE AUTHOR

K. M. Steele holds a PhD in English Literature from Macquarie University. Her debut novel, *Return to Tamarlin*, was published in 2017. Her second novel, *Hunt for the Virgin Rainbow*, is the first book in the *Mallory Cash* series and was published in 2021. *Race for the Topaz Stallion* (2024) is the second book of the series. Steele also has articles, reviews, essays, poetry, and short stories published in various journals, including: *Australian Book Review, Australian ejournal of Theology, Colloquy,M Transnational Literature*, and *Antipodes*.

To follow K. M. Steele, and hear about her upcoming
releases, including the third book in the
Mallory Cash series,
register for the newsletter at
www.hawkeyebooks.com.au
or follow her @KMSteele.author.

I love writing fiction and I aim to entertain you. If you liked
what you read today, could I ask you to leave a positive review
or tell your friends about this book on your favourite online
forum, and Goodreads?
Book reviews can make or break a book.

Hunt for the Virgin Rainbow and *Race for the Topaz Stallion* are
available at www.hawkeyebooks.com.au and all good bookstores
and libraries.

If you enjoyed *Race for the Topaz Stallion*,
we believe you'll also enjoy:

The Ghost Train and the Scarlet Moon by Jack Roney
Steve Hart: The Last Kelly Standing by Peter Long
What If You Fly by Camille Booker
New Year's Eve by Sarah Todman